Light Brights
&
Darkies

SHAIDA ESCOFFERY

ISBN: 0692222391
ISBN-13: 978-0692222393

DEDICATION

This book is dedicated to all women, especially those of color who have ever felt less than because of the shade of their skin. You are all beautiful, light or dark, and worth more than rubies.

CONTENTS

ACKNOWLEDGMENTS

I'm so blessed to feel beautiful because I know how fearfully and wonderfully God has made me. I have not always had this knowledge. I thank God for teaching me what I needed to know. This book would not have existed without the love of God being present in my life.

A Special thank you must be given to my parents Randy and Karen Escoffery, my most trusted readers. To my brother DJ, and my friends Timothy and Darian for all their support. To Kayla, Eboni and Atara, thank you for helping me name the characters. My church family, you guys are the best.

To Katherine, Tyler, Kelleigh, Rachel, Amy, Kristin, Kasey, Renee, Jeanine and Janice. I don't even think you all are aware of the path of self-acceptance and love you set me on. I am forever grateful for one summer that changed everything. Dr. Patti Rose, you taught me how to love all things black. Thank you for expanding my thoughts and opinions.

My family in Jamaica, New York, Texas and Florida. My grandparents, aunts, uncles and cousins. Love you all. Thank you for supporting me. Patrick, thank you for always making my books look good.

To the University of Miami, you made me grow. I am a Cane for life.

"It is not our differences that divide us. It is our inability to recognize, accept, and celebrate those differences."

Audre Lorde

1 REMINISCE

The sound of Lion King played in the background as I looked down at Nadia sleeping on the couch. Her chest rose and fell and her hair was beginning to come undone. As I lifted her into my arms I felt a slicing...no it was more of a tearing. I looked down at my arms to see that my skin had broken. I groaned and moved quietly to her bedroom and set her on the bed. My arms were stinging. I got a blanket and placed it over her before turning out the lights and going into my bedroom, I turned the corner into the master bedroom and raced to my bathroom. Getting a washcloth out, I wet it and then pressed it to the first tear on the crook of my arm. I closed my eyes and let my tears finally spill over.

"I haven't seen you in years!" Zoe said, as I walked into her office a week later. The open windows showcased the Miami skyline; its white high-rises against the blue of the ocean.

"I know," I said, running my hand on her nameplate that read, "Zoe Daniels, Attorney at Law".

She looked at me and smiled. "A lot has changed hasn't it?"

"Definitely. You're an attorney and most people forget my real name and just call me 'doc' all the time."

Zoe's a statuesque beauty, her skin a light caramel color. We were best friends in college and then after when we both moved onto grad school, our conversations just became more infrequent until she only became a person I'd text on holidays in a chain message.

"I haven't seen you since the wedding, how

long has it been, three years?" Zoe asked.

"Four," I corrected.

Her eyes registered sadness in them. Weariness. Zoe took my hand, and looked at my ring. "I never noticed it before, it's purple?"

"Yeah, it's an amethyst. I wanted to be different, so Sean made sure it was different. I love it."

"Yeah, you were kind of surrounded by family and other friends on your big day, so I couldn't get the details. Oh man, I wish I could've been there to see that love story unfold. You would've jumped on my bed and said 'Zo, so I met this guy...'" She created a little table with her hands, resting her chin on it, batting her lashes.

I giggled. She was right. That's how it would've been eleven years ago.

In 2008, I was in my first year of residency in the oncology ward when I met Sean. I knocked gently on the door and walked in. The room was the same light green color I'd seen in the other rooms, with the green damask wallpaper on the bottom, separated by the white wood trim. Sean was asleep in a bedside chair, his mouth wide open. His best friend Jordan was in the bed, sitting up, flipping in between watching CSI, Lost, 24, and then settling on The Office.

"He never leaves your side, does he?" I asked Jordan.

"Nope. Brotherly love, Doc." Jordan's hair had been shaved now and all that remained were his gaunt figure and piercing blue eyes.

He and Sean always made me smile. Even with Jordan's Chronic Myelogenous Leukemia diagnosis, they still managed to have a sense of humor. I smiled and moved to look at his monitor. His blood pressure was a bit low, not too bad though. I looked at the chart the nurse just gave me of his temperature. 100.4. Still high.

"You guys are closer than my sister and I."

Sean began to stir; he wiped drool from his

mouth and sat up, looking wide-eyed at me.

"Don't worry, nothing to be embarrassed about, it's just me."

"Yeah, just the doctor he's always so eager to see," Jordan said, grinning mischievously at Sean.

Sean returned the gesture, rolling his eyes. "Sorry, Dr. Palmer. Jordan is a bit loopy on those pain meds."

"Oh, I'm feeling fine. I've just been having these epiphanies. Life is too short and you shouldn't waste opportunities. So, Sean are you gonna ask out Dr. Palmer or what?"

Both Sean and I froze. I blushed and looked down. Sean was cute, but as horrible as this may sound, Sean wasn't the ideal boyfriend for me at the time. He was cute and he seemed like he was a lot of fun. But, maybe he'd do better for someone who was lighter than me. His cocoa colored skin would mix with my own and then what hope would a child of mine have? My son would always be seen as "threatening" or "menacing" and my daughter would be a "tar baby". No, Sean wouldn't do.

"He doesn't make six figures, but he's got a lot going for him. He's a high school history teacher. Got voted teacher of the year," Jordan continued.

"You did?" I asked.

"I did," Sean said, scratching his head and looking away. I could tell he probably wanted to strangle Jordan for this.

"What kind of history?"

"US Government and African- American History."

"Sweet," I said, although at the time I didn't really mean it. I mean I could go out with this guy, but I probably shouldn't get too attached to someone I wouldn't have a future with. I was 27, my biological clock was ticking.

I took my stethoscope and started to listen to Jordan's heart. I probably needed to calm my own heartbeat before I did this. Everything sounded good, his heartbeat was a bit faint, but the monitor was reading that he was doing alright. "So what did you have in mind?" I asked Sean.

"Excuse me?"

"For the date? What did you have in mind?" One date wouldn't hurt. I hadn't been on a date in such a long time. I knew it was a bit selfish, but it beat sitting at home all the time. One date and then I'd tell him it wasn't going to work out. Everyone deserved one chance.

He smiled. "Something fun."

"Hmmm. Fun as in dinner and a movie?"

"How about you two go to the Fair?" Jordan said.

"I love the Fair. Haven't been there in years."

"Well, then the Fair it is." Jordan said, while Sean looked at him with annoyance.

I grinned at Sean. "Be warned. I ride everything. Even the roller coasters."

Sean nodded in my direction and smirked. "I'll remember that." He stepped closer to me. "Before Jordan can make any further moves for me, Dr. Palmer, I think I should at least know your first name before I ask for your number."

I remember thinking he had the nicest smile. My parents would like that his hair was closely cut, his moustache and goatee well groomed. Mum would say that he looked respectable. No, she would say that he looks like "him have sense". I looked at him and answered, "Anaya."

A week later, I was grinning as I looked outside the windshield of Sean's Explorer at the Ferris Wheel towering into the sky and hearing the screams of people on rides that were flipping them upside down. Sean parked the car and turned off the engine. We'd been talking to each other non-stop on the phone all week. This wasn't going according to plan. He'd ask about Jamaica, college, and he certainly wasn't stupid. We talked about everything from politics to healthcare. The more I talked to him, the more I liked him. He needed to say something dumb or insensitive--- and fast. He was making it too hard to back out of this when someone better came along. But, every time we talked the conversation flowed so easily, and I was beginning to think he got more attractive since I'd last seen him.

"You look excited," Sean said.

I turned to him. "And you look nervous."

"I'm good."

"Are you sure?"

He sighed and leaned back. "I don't really go on rides."

I laughed. "Are you afraid?"

He gripped the steering wheel. "A little." He put his head in his hands. "This is embarrassing."

This was embarrassing for him, but I thought it was a little cute too. "Come on, it's not so bad."

Funny thing was I found myself having to utter those words again when Sean hurled all of the elephant ear into the trash can after we went on the Tilt-A-Whirl.

"I'll get you some water," I said, heading to the concession stand.

When I got there, the guy at the counter looked past me at Sean. "Your boyfriend looks like he's in bad shape."

I should've said that he wasn't really my boyfriend; in fact this was the perfect opportunity to dump this guy. Our first date and he vomits. But, I felt a sense of loyalty to him. I mean I'd pressured him to go on the ride. "Yeah, rides aren't really his thing."

He chuckled and handed me the water. I walked over to Sean, who was now sitting down on a bench nearby. He wouldn't even look at me.

"Here," I said, handing him the water and sitting beside him.

He twisted the cap and gulped down some. "So it's safe to say this is probably the worst date you've ever had."

I leaned back and laughed. "Close. But, no, not the worst."

He raised his eyebrows. "Girl, what kind of dates do you go on?"

"Not many. But there was a guy in college who took me out and on our way to the restaurant we got pulled over. Turns out, he took his brother's car without asking. And his brother reported it stolen. I almost went to jail that night. My best friend at the time had to pick me up."

Sean laughed. "I should've asked if you had a record before we went out."

I punched him in the shoulder playfully. "And I shouldn't have insisted you go on the ride. You were screaming louder than me."

He covered his face and groaned. "Don't tell Jordan."

"Hmm, you know that's very tempting. Jordan and I both love a good laugh."

Sean shook his head. "That's cold."

"I won't tell Jordan."

"Thanks. Maybe we should head back to the car," he said, getting up.

"We're gonna leave so soon?" Even though this place was filled with teenagers and bits of popcorn, elephant ears, and empty fresh squeezed lemonade cups littering the floor, I actually liked the county fair. It reminded me of my first year in this country when I'd come with my aunt's church youth group. I was young and full of hope with the prospects of being in America.

"Yeah, I figured you'd want to be put out of

your misery."

"Misery loves company. Maybe we can do something else that doesn't involve spinning fifty feet in the air."

Sean crossed his arms over his chest. "Ok, what did you have in mind?"

"Something fun."

He smiled. "Alright Anaya. Let me go to my car and get a toothbrush or something. Not trying to have vomit breath all night."

We started walking back towards the car. "You have toothbrushes in your car?"

"Yeah. Well, when Jordan first started chemo he'd just randomly get sick. So I started keeping a few packs of toothbrushes, toothpaste, and mouthwash for him. Didn't want my boy walking around with yuck mouth."

I looked at him for a while.

"What?"

"I just think that's really...nice. I mean it takes a special person to take care of his best friend like that."

"You take care of sick patients everyday. That takes a special person. Strong person."

"No, I think the real strength is in the people like Jordan who have to live with cancer and hold on to hope that they'll overcome the disease. And friends and family who believe with them."

We were almost to the car when he turned to me and asked, "Why did you decide to be an oncologist?"

I didn't really know what to tell him. When I'd first started I wanted to save people. Not to mention everyone was so proud of me. Nothing pleases a Jamaican family more than to know their child has some fancy occupation or found Jesus. Prestige and money may have been a factor, but I honestly loved taking care of people. If I didn't make any money, I'd still do it. I thought maybe I'd find a cure for cancer. But, things didn't work like that, and only one year into being a full-fledged doctor I was watching the old and the young die. "I wanted to give people hope for a healthier and full life."

We got to his Explorer and he clicked for it to

open. The trunk of the truck lifted and he went to retrieve the toothbrush and toothpaste. He found a water bottle inside and brushed. I sat in the back of the truck looking outside at the Miami night sky. He finished up brushing and then moved inside to sit next to me.

"You know if I wasn't mistaken I'd say you probably started medicine to save people and then when you got into oncology you realized maybe you couldn't, so you settled for just making their last few days on Earth tolerable."

"What makes you think that?" I said, looking over at him, his face still overlooking the sky.

"Just a good guess," he said, glancing over at me. Sean's smile was always a little lopsided, but I loved it that way. The side where his smile was widest was where one dimple was deeper than the other.

"I still haven't told you if you're right."

"Am I?"

I sighed. "I guess you are. But, I'm not supposed to say things like that considering your best friend is my patient."

He sighed deeply. "Jordan doesn't really accept death. He won't let me or his parents even entertain the thought." He turned to me.

"I don't think I've ever seen his parents."

"Sure you did. They were there the last time you came in."

The only people that had been there were a tall black man and a middle aged black woman who still had an athletic build.

He read the confusion on my face. "Jordan is adopted. His parents are black."

"Oh, I'm sorry, I assumed they were *your* parents."

"Nah, close enough though. I crashed at their place pretty much most of college."

"Wow, I feel like I just failed the cultural competency portion of my medical knowledge."

Sean laughed. "Just as long as you don't give up on Jordan."

"Between you and I, I think Jordan will be just fine in no time at all."

"What makes you say that?"

"Cancer can claim anyone it chooses. But, I've often seen that the ones who live and laugh despite it, have the longest lifespan."

Sean nodded and placed his hand on mine. "Thanks."

"Just being honest."

He gave a faint smile. "Do all Jamaicans actually pronounce the 'h' in honest?"

I pinched him. "Are you making fun of my accent?"

"I actually think it's nice. I hope it doesn't wear off."

I blushed despite myself.

"So what's this fun thing you had in mind?" he asked.

I smirked. "Ever played laser tag?"

We were geared up with our vest and guns. The room was lit in blue florescent lighting, the targets in neon yellows, greens, and pinks. We were battling a group of ten year olds. We raced into the arena taking cover behind walls. We took down a few of the 5th graders and then we dodged behind the same wall together. If you were shot five times, you were out. I shot one of the boys before his little girlfriend shot me back. I saw her stick out her tongue, before I ran to take cover. Sean was there and he smiled, his white teeth florescent under the lighting. I stared and laughed.

"What?"

"Your teeth are glow in the dark."

I didn't realize I'd said something cute or romantic because he just leaned over and kissed me. Right in the middle of our battle against the 10 year olds and before I knew it we were surrounded, our chests vibrating because we'd gotten shot more than five times each. And then came the sound of the kids' resounding "ewww!"

And Sean asked. "Are you having fun?"

Zoe was smiling down at me now. "That's so cute... in a kind of gross way. You kissed a guy who vomited."

"He brushed!" I said, laughing and then taking a seat. Her office was decked out and I looked around at the cherry wood and the mounted degrees on her wall. Zoe must be getting *paid*.

"You and your husband are nerds," she said, between laughs. She sat down in her leather chair and leaned her head back and sighed. "I should've been there to hear all of this before."

"Yeah, after college you kind of checked out."

"Law school was no joke."

"Neither was med school."

Zoe swallowed and looked serious. "I didn't deserve it, but thanks for the invite to the wedding. It really was beautiful."

I remembered that day like it was yesterday. The day I changed from being Dr. Palmer to Dr. Blake. It was a beach wedding in the Keys, with red everywhere. Red roses, carnations, anemones, and freesias. I didn't like the planning process so I'd hired someone, and it was a day most women dream of. My mom and dad had attended the wedding, my mom shelling out every dime she had on an expensive dress made for her in Kingston. My brother and my sister's presence were missing. My parents liked Sean. I'd actually married an American, and it wasn't a business marriage. According to everyone back home, I was lucky. But, "lawd yuh kids ah go black. Hopefully dem will tek after dem granny."

I remember dancing with my husband on our wedding day and replaying those words in my head. I breathed a silent prayer that if my kids didn't come out light then I didn't want to have any at all.

I cleared my throat. "That's actually what I came to talk to you about. Sean wants a divorce."

Zoe leaned forward. "He's filed papers?"

"Not yet. But, he's not living with me anymore," I said, my eyes misting.

"What's going on Naya? Is he having an affair?"

I shook my head. "No. Sean wouldn't do that.

He's very faithful. We just had a son. He took him with him."

"And why would he do that?"

"Because, he doesn't believe I can care for him."

Zoe looked to me for clarity.

"I've, um, been having difficulty bonding with my son."

Zoe's eyes widened. "You mean post partum?"

"No, not necessarily. I'm just disappointed in..." I swallowed. "I thought my son would be different. Would... look different."

She breathed deeply. "I don't know..."

"I figured you were the only person I could come to about this. When we were in college you'd tan and I'd do the exact opposite and I figured that you'd understand."

"Yes, but this is a *baby*. I didn't think all of this would continue and you'd hold onto this."

"Look, I don't want to be vilified. I just need legal help. I need a friend-"

"I don't know how to help you with this."

"I'm sick," I blurted out.

Zoe froze. "My skin is breaking again. I just had to remove some melanomas. There's no sign of cancer anywhere else, but I'm having trouble keeping up. I can't go into the sun; I can't do simple things without bruising or my skin tearing. Sean doesn't know it's this bad. He's been begging me to stay off those creams for years and I wouldn't listen." I got up from my chair. "We argue about everything and when it boils down to it, the argument stems from my insecurities. From my skin."

"You can't be serious."

"Look at my skin! It looks terrible and all I keep hoping for is to look like you!" Tears wet my face.

"That's crazy."

"Is it?" I said, looking into her dark brown eyes. "You tan to look like me. But, you never will. Maybe you should let me check you out. Verify if you're healthy."

"Did you come in here for consultation or to lecture me?"

I swallowed. "I came here for your help. I don't really have many friends. Correction, I don't have *any* friends besides my husband."

"So what do you want me to do?"

"Well, I need a lawyer for my impending divorce. My three-year-old niece is staying with me permanently. I need some help with her while I try to get some help, some medical care."

"You need a roommate?"

"Roommate, nurse, friend. Whatever title works best for you."

She rubbed her forehead. "Wow. This is certainly a reunion."

"You always said I was full of surprises."

Zoe nodded and turned her chair sideways and looked to her left out the window. "I had a melanoma a year ago."

I walked past her desk and stood in front of her. She wouldn't look into my face. "They caught it early and cut it off. Told me to be more careful and stop tanning."

"Did you?"

She looked at me now. "No."

2 MANGO TIME

I am the middle child. My older brother by two years, Delroy, was my hero and my younger sister by one year, Julie...well I always did think that she was a little crazy. I don't know what my mother was thinking naming her after a type of mango. Mum said I was born in a zinc shack in Linstead, Jamaica, before we upgraded to the two room flat when I was 12. She was confident she would die during that labor. It wasn't so much the pain, but the fact that it was so long. My parents loved me, that much I did know as a child. But, I was unaware that there were people in the country who lived in beautiful mansions in the hills. I assumed everyone had a zinc house that needed repairing every couple days to keep out the rain.

Life was hard, but life was full of simple pleasures. The sunrise and sunset. Picking mangoes, cherries, plums, anything we could get our hands on. I used to love juneplums and soursop. It was what I would look forward to each day, getting juneplums and soursop from some person's tree. Once some obeah woman cursed my brother, sister and I for stealing her fruit. We laughed at her and screamed "Gway!" But that night we all couldn't sleep cause we were afraid we'd wake up with a pig nose or missing thumbs. We never stole from her again. Life was beautiful back then, now that I think about it. I wish I never harbored such horrible thoughts about myself.

Going through primary and high school was a challenge. We were always short on money for books and uniforms. Roy, Julie, and I would always get teased about our clothes and they would happily fight. Poor pickney dem. Dutty gyal. Mi bet seh yuh baggie have hole. I'd regularly hear that. But, I didn't really have it in me to fight. One hit and I was ready

27

to surrender and go home crying. They ended up having to fight for me most times. Once, Roy nearly killed a boy for pushing me up against a wall and trying to touch me. That was the first time I actually saw pure rage. The flared nostrils, the bloodied hands, the eyes that were so red you'd think he was crying. My brother permanently looked like that until he left us. I would've never imagined that anger would rule the boy who used to bring Julie and I flowers for our birthday and go and pick fruit for us for no reason. He would've made some woman happy.

By the time I was twelve and hit high school, my brother had dropped out of school and gone and become a gunman. Daddy tossed him out the second he found his stash of ganja and his gun. The only people who should have guns were police and soldiers. Roy never argued with him, just picked up some of his stuff, tossed it in a pillowcase and left. Mum cried for a week. Roy was her favorite. He would come home sometimes bringing money, food and clothes with him when Daddy wasn't around.

Mum would make him banana porridge and cook him some ackee and saltfish. Daddy eventually caught on when he'd come home to the smell of bananas in the air and the onions in the ackee. Only Roy liked onions and everyone knew that.

Julie was the next to go. Mum found a miniskirt under her bed and started asking questions. Mum laced her with the belt for that. Julie told me not to say a word about the nights she'd slip out. Just tell her seh yuh nuh hear mi. I didn't know it then, but she was running around with grown men. Men from gangs. Men like my brother. Roy killed the man she was seeing. Walked right in on them and shot him. Took my sister back home to my mother. But, Julie wouldn't stay. She was a "woman". A 14-year-old woman. A week later, the man's gang shot Roy. Cornered him while he was walking to his place one night. 19 bullet wounds. 8 of them fatal. Julie, came back home then, but my mother cussed her. Julie was only half way up the dirt road when my mother saw her and raced out the house yelling, "Nuh come in here! You harlot, you murderer! Ah you kill Roy! Ah you kill him!" She turned back down the dirt road and walked back to wherever she came from. That was the last time I saw my sister. Until I received a visit from a social worker two weeks ago asking me to take temporary custody of my three-year-old niece I wasn't even aware I had.

I was my parents' only hope. It was evident in the extra money Daddy would save to get me good books for school. He didn't have two other children to waste money on anymore. Mum sewed me some more clothes and started to hot comb my hair more often. "Ya go be successful, yuh hear?" she'd say, bending over the back of my head, running the hot comb through my hair while I flinched, scared each time I felt the heat and heard the frying of my hair. But after I finished high school at 17, I left her. I couldn't manage to stay in that home anymore. Not when everywhere I'd go I'd remember Roy climbing the trees for me while Julie twirled around singing "Mango time". I moved out to Kingston. There were buildings and factories. Not like back home. I called my aunt in Miami religiously, begging her to help me come to America so I could go to school and make something of myself. In the meantime, I found a job at a cell phone company, and at nights I could easily find a party and dance away my homesickness.

It was at those parties I started getting the comments about my tar-like skin. I'd heard them before, and they'd hurt, especially when I'd seen that my sister wasn't nearly as dark as I was. But, now I felt it affected the way men saw me. "Yuh need fi do some toning Naya," was all I'd hear. So, I saved enough money and got myself some bleach and a few other skin lightening products, like my friend Marcia had told me to. And I went over her house and watched her mix them all up into a big jar. I had to undress and then she smeared it over my skin, and it burned a bit. She rubbed it all over and then wrapped me in saran wrap. She told me to put on tons of layers, even gloves. I asked her why. She told me, "Yuh ah go sweat and the skin ah go come off like a snake ah shed him skin. When yuh see di light skin under all a dat tar, yuh nah go waan stop bleach."

And she was right. Even when I moved up to the United States, with a student visa, to live with my Aunt Deloris when I turned 18, I still bleached, which she hated. I couldn't go hardcore like I'd done in Jamaica and shed my skin, but the creams worked just fine. I treated them like lotions. My aunt would tell me I had lost my blooming mind. Give me scriptures on how I was "fearfully and wonderfully made". But, I kept at it. No one could convince me that what I was doing wouldn't make me more beautiful. I used to imagine my skin would look like Julie's did, a nice cinnamon color. Mum used to love Julie's skin; she said only one of us had gotten her complexion. I think maybe that's why it hurt Mum so much that Julie had begun to sell herself. Her one pretty child was a "lady of the night". I'd hum "mango time" and rub that poison all over myself, thinking that one day I'd find Julie and she could come live with me once I started making money. My skin never did look like Julie's.

My aunt worked at the university in Miami and

gotten me a free ride because of some family tuition program thing. It was perhaps the best thing to happen to me. I stayed on campus and eventually met up with Zoe. I loved, but envied her. Such a tall girl with all those beautiful curls. She was so light that if she straightened her hair most people probably wouldn't have thought she was black. Yet, nearly every day she stepped out into the glorious Miami sun and baked there. Her gripe was that she unevenly tanned because she had to keep her top on. So on the weekends she'd run off to the nude beach.

"Let's get a place off campus." Zoe said, as our junior year approached. And we did. Her parents could afford to spot her the extra money and she was able to tan in peace at her own leisure. And I was able to continue to bleach.

After a while, my skin got even lighter, but it was an ashy color, like wood that's been sanded, but not polished. It became so sensitive I couldn't go out in the sun without a hoodie or an umbrella. Felt like I was catching on fire anytime the sun hit my skin. And then my skin started to burst open, if I moved too fast, the skin would just rip. The doctor said I had weakened it with the chemicals. Zoe got scared and told me to lay off the cream. Tanning was normal. Bleaching was not. As I applied for med school I did stop using it and after some time, my skin took on back its natural tone, slowly but surely that deep mahogany skin came back. My skin was never as soft and supple as it once was, but with cocoa butter and some extra care, my skin started to look youthful again, the only reminder of the past had been in the scars left from the tearing of my skin earlier. When Sean would ask where the scars on the inside of my elbows, knees and on my hips came from, I'd just tell him childhood scars from climbing trees or playing outside.

Even with the commentary from people about how my children would look, it wasn't until two years into my marriage that I'd started bleaching again. Sean and I had been out for dinner when we ran into an old girlfriend of his. She was gorgeous. Everything I wasn't. Tall, light, a head full of long curls. She could've been Zoe's sister. And can you imagine that this woman just looked at me with disdain and was openly flirting with my husband? He didn't flirt back. Probably because I would've killed him. He stood up for me and dodged her. But, when I came home nothing he said could erase her memory from my head. Maybe if I went back to the bleach I'd look better. I just wouldn't go so hardcore this time. Just a little bit.

I didn't tell Sean at first. He eventually put things together when he found my stash of creams. He'd been asking for a while why my skin looked a bit different. Imagine a man who dedicates his life to studying the significance of Black people having a wife who was trying to eradicate her own blackness. I stopped using the creams again, but each time my skin returned to normal, I became extremely insecure, always thinking he was looking at another woman.

"Why don't you just go marry some yellow or white woman!" I'd yell when we got into arguments.

I didn't want to have kids, even though I knew Sean loved kids. He wanted a girl. I *never* wanted a girl. I would never want her to be dark like me. So I stayed on birth control, even when I'd told him I'd come off so we could try to conceive.

But the birth control had failed and I found myself suffering from continual morning sickness before I acknowledged the evident. I was pregnant. Despite all the cocoa butter I'd put on, I still got a bunch of stretch marks all over because my skin wasn't as strong as it used to be. Still, I'd forced myself to be excited by imagining myself with baby that had escaped my fate and had a head full of curls and skin the color of cinnamon. But, at nights I'd have nightmares that after my labor I'd see the tell tale signs of dark ears and knuckles on my newborn. And just like that, when Jeremy was handed to me those dark ears and knuckles were present. I smiled and cried in front of my husband and midwife, but no one knew that those were tears of sadness and not of joy.

Still, I love my son. Jeremy is a sweet baby. He hardly fusses, only when he's hungry. But, as the months went by his skin took on the same color as mine. I was horrified. I remember rocking him to sleep and silently crying. He looked like me. Most days I couldn't wait for Sean to come home so he could care for Jeremy. I'd pump and then give Jeremy the bottle. Breastfeeding him would allow him to be too close. I barely even wanted to breastfeed. I wanted to stop so I could bleach again.

"What's your problem Anaya?" Sean asked after I had left Jeremy in his crib crying. Sean had just come out of the shower and I was on the recliner in our room. "Don't you hear him crying?"

"Let him self soothe he'll be fine."

Sean narrowed his eyes. "I swear, something is wrong with you."

"Don't swear," I said, just sitting there. "Nothing is wrong with me."

He disappeared into the nursery and got Jeremy out of his crib. "Do you have a bottle made for him?"

"No, I don't think so. He eats so much."

"Well, I think he might be hungry. Can you see if by some miracle he'll latch on?"

"So he can make me sore? No, thanks."

I could see Sean's breathing become heavy. "Are you having post partum? What? What is it?!"

"It's nothing," I sneered.

He stared at me for a while incredulously. "I'm going to get him some food and I'm going to take him out to the park or something. I think you need some time alone," He said, turning away from me.

"You're not taking my child to the park so that he can get even darker than he already is."

Sean stopped in his tracks and turned around, his hand on Jeremy's head, rocking him. "What did you say?"

I sat down and sighed looking out the window. "Nothing."

"Is that why?..."

I looked him in his eyes. "Jeremy needs to stay inside," I said, quietly.

"Why? So that he can be stuck with a mother that's completely detached from him?"

"Shut up!" I yelled, which started Jeremy's

wailing again. "I love my son."

"No, you don't. You don't want to bond with him. You don't even smile with him."

I felt heat rush my face and my eyes water. "How can I smile when I look at him?"

I could see the betrayal and pain on his face. "He's your son. He's a part of you."

"That's the problem Sean! He's too much like me! Maybe if-"

"I'm not listening to this," he said, walking to the kitchen. I followed him as he got some food for Jeremy, avoiding my eyes as he began to feed him.

"You're not understanding."

"You're right. I don't understand. Would you like it if he were lighter? Would that make things better for you?"

"Yes," I said, as if that was the simplest thing in the world.

Sean's jaw was tense. "That's it. We gotta get out of here."

He moved past me with Jeremy. I didn't follow him. By the time he came back he had a duffel bag and Jeremy's baby bag.

"Why do you need all of that for the park?"

"I think you need some time to yourself. To think. To get a clue Anaya!"

Months of fighting had come to a boiling point and all I could do was stammer and tell him not to take Jeremy. But I couldn't take back what I'd said. I sat there on the rocking chair in the nursery, rocking back and forth aimlessly as he took our child, and left.

They say we all cope and grieve in different ways. The first day I sat there, convinced that once Sean cooled off that he'd be back home. Two more days went by and he still hadn't showed or called. I went out to the store and bought back my creams and sat there and bleached the way I used to in Jamaica, saran wrap, skin shedding and all. God, I'm a terrible person.

Then irony hit me like a ton of bricks when I heard from the social worker and three days later my niece was dropped off to my home. An unfit mother being handed over a child by another unfit

LIGHT BRIGHTS & DARKIES

mother. It was funny in a dark, twisted way. I remember thinking that my niece was a cute little thing. She didn't look like Julie to be honest. Her skin was the color of milk chocolate, her eyes almond shaped and brown, her hair pulled back into one large puff. Scary thing was she looked like...me. Julie had died two years ago from a cocaine overdose, so I wondered why was my niece just being given to me.

Five years ago in 2009, a couple of months before I married Sean, I visited Julie in prison. I had no idea she had even been in the US all this time. She'd gotten locked up for having a couple grams of cocaine on her. At the time I hadn't even wanted to know what she could possibly be doing with it.

"How did you get your papers to live here Julie?" I asked.

She shrugged. "Business marriage."

I shook my head. "Where's your husband?"

"Like I said, it was a business marriage. Him nuh deal wid mi and mi nuh deal wid him."

"How long is your sentence?"

"Judge give mi one year. But, dem seh di prison

overcrowded."

I nodded. "You should get clean."

"Mi deh inna jail. I'm clean."

My annoyance flared. "Weh you want mi fi tell Daddy and Mum?"

"You can tell them whatever you want."

"And break their hearts?"

I'd broken past her armor. "Don't tell them anything right now. Make them think I'm still in Jamaica doing whatever."

"Why don't you go back home?"

"People down there will be looking for me."

I gritted my teeth. "What did you do?"

"I killed the man who killed Roy."

I exhaled. "You're insane."

Julie laughed and I stared. "Anaya. I've made some real bad choices. But, at least I've lived. You work and work and you don't live." She looked at my hand. "You got engaged?"

"Yeah, you'll miss the wedding."

She nodded and gave a faint smile. "Who's your maid of honor?"

"I don't have one."

"I'm sorry I can't be there."

I looked away. "Me too."

"Is he handsome?"

"Of course."

"Good, cause mi nuh accept ugly people in dis family."

I laughed at that. "Julie that's messed up."

"Do you have any kids yet?" she asked.

"No, not yet and I'm in no rush."

"Me neither, well not yet." She smiled. "But, if I do and anything ever happened to me, promise me you'll raise my kids. Just like they you're your own." Silence filled the air and her chin quivered, her eyes glassy. "Promise me."

"Don't have any until you're ready."

She huffed. "I'll try." She stared into my eyes. "Do you promise?"

I nodded. "I've been saving you since we were kids. I don't think I can stop now. I promise."

She moistened her lip with her tongue and nodded.

"Julie, there's something you're not telling me."

She scratched behind her ear. "I've given you enough bad news to last a lifetime."

I reached out for her hand. The guard called out to me. "No touching."

I moved my hand. "You just came back and now you'll be gone again."

Tears streamed down her face. "Please don't do this, you know I'm no good with goodbyes."

"I want you to do two things for me."

She shrugged. "Anything."

"If anything happens to you, make sure you have them call me. Leave my number on you, whatever, but I want to know that you're safe."

"I can't guarantee safety, but for as long you don't hear from me that means I'm alive."

I nodded.

"What was the second thing?"

"Sing for me again. Sing Mango time for me."

Julie smiled and sang softly, "Mi nuh drink coffee tea mango time." I started to clap the familiar reggae beat. I opened my mouth and sang with her. "Care how nice it may be mango time." Our voices rose in harmony as the guard came over and told her time was up. Julie didn't resist, but never stopped singing as she got up and started walking back to her cell.

"In the heat of the mango crop/When di fruit dem a ripe an drop." She reached the exit of the visiting room and waved to me, all the while singing, "Wash your pot turn dem down mango time."

3 TRANSITIONS

Two days after my trip to Zoe's office, the phone rang at two in the morning. "Hello," I said, groggily.

"What happens if I say yes?"

"Are you?"

"Yeah, I am. I owe you. I can't just leave you alone like that."

"Ok, well then we'll need to also figure out a payment for your-"

"I don't want any money Anaya."

I sat up in bed and turned on the bedside lamp. "What about for your law services?"

"I don't need any money because I won't be

representing you."

"What? Why not?"

"Because you're not getting a divorce. I'm gonna get you back together with your husband."

I scoffed at her. "And just how are you going to do that?"

"Do you want your husband back?"

"Yes, but-

"Give me his number, I promise I'll make it happen."

"Zo, I don't think you can just call a man and demand he take back his wife."

"Why can't I? I'm trained in the art of persuasion. I handle divorces and settlements. I'm used to seeing behave badly. I know the million reasons people break up. So inversely, I know the things that can keep them together. So you and I are going to have a long talk about everything that went wrong. And then you're going to give me his number or address, whichever works better for him."

"You're something else," I said, rubbing my eyes.

"I know."

"I'm not working right now so anytime you want to come over is fine with me. I drop off Nadia off to daycare by 8:30 and go pick her back up at three."

"I'll come over around noon tomorrow. And I'll bring some of my things with me."

We were both silent for a little. "Thank you Zo. This means a lot."

"You're welcome. Goodnight, I'll see you in the morning."

"Goodnight."

At seven in the morning I nudged Nadia awake. It's been a month since Sean and Jeremy have been gone. It's been three weeks since Nadia came to live with me and it's taking me a while to adjust to having a toddler. But, it did seem to fill a bit of the ache of missing the feel of Jeremy, even though Nadia didn't smell like baby lotion. Nadia was also getting adjusted to me, considering she'd been in a foster home for two years. Every time I thought about it, I just got mad again thinking that two years ago they'd been able to inform me that my sister died. I'd gone back to Jamaica and buried her, but no one had bothered to find out that she'd had a daughter.

"Hey, it's time to get up."

Nadia whimpered, I picked her up out of the bed and walked with her in my arms to the bathroom. As much as my arms were feeling the strain, I didn't want to demand she walk. I started to get her ready for a bath.

"Auntie Naya, I want to stay home with you."

"How about I take you to school and pick you up earlier today?" I said, as I soaped up her arms.

"Ok."

"And we can watch princess movies."

She smiled. "I want to look like Cinderella."

"You are a princess like Cinderella," I said, as I washed her off.

"No, I don't have yellow hair and my skin is brown."

I froze and put down the showerhead. "Sweetie, Cinderella is beautiful and so are you." I really did think Nadia was a cute kid. Beautiful, even though she didn't look like Julie. I swallowed hard thinking of Jeremy. I missed him in moments like this, or when I realized there were no sounds of cooing or need to use baby lotion.

"Ok," she said, looking down into the water.

"How about we watch Tianna tonight?"

"The man with scary masks in the movie scares me."

"Ok, then we'll watch Finding Nemo or Lion King."

"That's not a princess movie."

"But they're good."

"Can we watch Pocahontas?"

"Ok. Pocahontas it is."

At noon Zoe knocked on my door. I opened for her and helped her carry in two rolling suitcases and she still had two duffel bags with her.

"Goodness, Zoe, you still over pack."

"Old habits die hard," she said, looking around. "You have a beautiful home."

It was a nice home. Sean and I had bought it a

year ago; he'd wanted more space for when we had kids and a big backyard so he could build them a swing set. Eventually we'd settled on a foreclosed home in the Gables that had a huge front lawn and backyard complete with a pool. It was too much space considering we had no kids. But, now with two kids, the extra space was nice. I stayed indoors most of the time, so I'd spent my time with the interior of the house making sure the walls in the living room were the perfect shade of marigold.

"Do you want something to eat?" I asked, as we made our way to the kitchen.

"Nope. Come on let's sit for a little bit."

I directed her to the living room.

"Relax," she said, making a show of breathing and letting down her shoulders.

I took a deep breath. "Ok. I'm relaxed."

"So how's it been taking care of a three year old?"

I chuckled. "Hard. I mean I just don't know a whole lot about toddlers. I feel like I'm playing catch up. I had to call a colleague who's a pediatrician for tips on how to make sure she doesn't wet the bed.

She talks a mile a minute and asks so many questions. I love it, but I miss..." I stopped. "When she and Jeremy come together it'll probably be madness."

Zoe looked at me knowingly and then lightly laughed. "What did I get myself into?"

"This morning she told me she wants to be like Cinderella."

"Then get her a costume or something."

"No, she wants to *look* like her. She wants to be white with blonde hair."

"And what did *you* tell her?"

"I was kind of taken aback by what she said. I mean does it really start that young Zo? I told her that she was beautiful the way she is and I suggested another movie for her to watch."

"Does she have dolls or movies of beautiful women that look like her?"

"No, um just one movie, but she says it's scary."

"We'll have to get her some books with some black princesses and some black dolls, Anaya."

"Do you think that will help?"

"Did you have that growing up?"

"Zoe, we couldn't afford that stuff. Now, my parents are getting older and can't work like they used to. They practically survive off the money I send them monthly."

"Well, now you can afford to get your children things. We should get her some today."

"Ok."

I looked outside at the sunny Miami day.

"And now for your marriage…"

"You don't waste any time do you?"

"You know I don't."

"What about it?"

"Was he unfaithful?"

"I already told you no."

"Just double checking. Were you?"

"Of course not."

"Were there financial problems?"

"Not really."

"What does he do for a living?"

"He just became a professor at the university two years ago."

"So two doctors living under the same roof." She tapped her fingers on the arm of the chair. "Did he complain about your work hours?"

"No, I work three days a week and those are the days he chooses to work so that we can spend our days off together."

"Do you two have sex? Regularly?"

"Zoe!"

"I'm your attorney and a friend. I'm going to have to know."

I eyed her before answering. "We did. But, um we've been kinda getting distant."

"Why?"

"Well, I just had a baby."

"Yeah, six months ago. Your point is?"

I rolled my eyes. "Like you've had any children to know about these things."

"I know that if you have an attractive husband, no physical problems or emotional problems, then sex after six to eight weeks isn't a problem. So tell me, which one was it, a physical or emotional problem?"

I narrowed my eyes at her. She didn't back down.

"Because I..." I fought to acknowledge the words.

"You what?"

"I won't let him."

"Why not?" Zoe said straightforwardly.

I looked down and cleared my throat. "I don't want to run the risk of getting pregnant again."

"Is this something you two have discussed?"

"We have," I sighed. "He wants at least three kids. But, I don't."

"Why not? Is it your career?"

I shook my head. "I'm afraid to have more kids."

Zoe looked confused and cocked her head to one side. "Afraid of the labor pains?"

"Well, yes. I mean that's a concern. But, it's not the reason. I don't want to have any more kids unless they're lighter. So I'm willing to adopt or-"

Zoe cleared her throat. "Anaya, please tell me you don't *actually* believe that?"

"You sound like Sean."

"You don't want to have kids because they'll be dark?"

"Go on any search engine and type in beautiful

women and tell me how many black women you see. Zoe, I want my children to have a chance."

"You want your children to be loved for their *skin*. That's wrong Naya. They should be loved because of who they are."

"Hardly anyone cares who you are deep down. Image *matters* Zoe. Do you know how hard I've had to fight to prove that I'm even half as intelligent as the rest of the world?"

Zoe leaned forward and stared into my eyes. "Anaya, this is crazy talk. You hear me? You're letting your *marriage* dissolve over self-esteem issues."

"Look at the kettle calling the pot black."

"What's that supposed to mean?"

I rolled my eyes. "Oh, Zoe, come on. You spent all of undergrad tanning your skin and looking for the darkest skinned boyfriend you could find. I don't even know what your natural skin looks like."

"I'm not ruining my life over that."

"You aren't?" I said, challenging her. "So that's why you had melanoma. And why you're almost thirty three and completely alone." Zoe folded her arms over her chest. I continued, "Maybe it's because you're searching for someone to make this "perfect" black child with you. Or maybe it's cause you really don't like yourself although women all over world would kill to look like you. Hell, I'd kill to look like you. You know how many opportunities are probably given to you because of your skin? Don't treat me like I'm some misnomer. If you got into a marriage, you'd be in the same predicament. You don't love yourself, neither of us do."

I couldn't tell whether she was going to explode and cuss me out or just pick up her bags and leave. Zoe swallowed. "Let's get one thing straight. I've worked hard to get to where I am. I am just as qualified as any other attorney. Don't *ever* question that. But with regard to other things you said, you're right. I'm not that different from you. The question still remains, are you going to let your marriage dissolve because of this? Are you willing to cite irreconcilable differences because of *this*?"

I was sobbing in front of Zoe as if eleven years

hadn't gone by. It suddenly hit me that it felt so strange to be this vulnerable. I could've called someone at the church, but I didn't. I was too afraid for someone to stand there and judge me or to spread that I was a crazy mother and a bad wife. "I am not. I just don't know fix this. Because I don't know how to fix me."

Zoe rested her hand on mine and then gathered me in an embrace. "I know I've always been the problem solver, but this time I don't know what to do either." She leaned back and looked at me. "We're in the same boat." I chuckled sardonically and she cradled my face in her hands. "But, we have to fix this Naya. You have to survive and take care of a son and a three-year-old little girl. Let's not forget, you have to repair things with your husband."

"And you?"

She smiled. "And I have to get myself checked out and stay away from tanning... and get a man."

We both laughed at that.

I wiped at my face and we rose up off the couch. "Now, missy you are not off the hook. I need your husband's contact information. His number. Do you know where he's staying?"

I went to the kitchen and grabbed an orange. "Yeah, with his best friend Jordan. Why?"

"Cause I'm going to pay him a visit within the week."

"And do what?"

"Tell him that his wife is ready to make amends and see her son. Your son needs his mother."

"He needs a more emotionally stable mother, which is why I haven't called Sean and begged to see him."

"We're going to work on it and I'm calling your husband."

"Zoe-"

"Do you want him filing papers or not?"

"I don't!"

"Well, then let me work my magic."

"Do *not* tell him about my skin."

"I think he should know that."

"Yes, but he should hear it from me."

She sighed. "True. Ok, I won't tell him you have

paper skin."

I peeled the orange, smelling the citrus scent filling my nostrils. "Let me clarify Zo. Do not tell him there's anything wrong with my skin, don't tell him it rips."

Zoe rolled her eyes. "Ok, I won't." She pulled back the blinds and looked out the window. "Gosh, look at that pool. I may wait a week or so. I want to enjoy this place before your husband moves back in and kicks me out."

"What makes you so sure he'll want to move back in?"

"If your husband even remotely still loves you, he'll want to come back. Trust me. Do you think your husband loves you?"

"I...I don't know. I just don't want him to suffer here with me anymore. I want to be healthy when he comes back."

Zoe came around and took the other half of my orange. "I agree. But, maybe he'll help you heal in ways you couldn't on your own."

4 INDEPENDENT WOMEN

Zoe's heels clicked along the floor as we walked through the toy store trying to pick up as many black dolls as we could. She was the only woman who'd wear a pants suit and heels anywhere even though she was already so tall. I'd stopped wearing tight clothing. It felt weird against my skin. Zoe had to reach to get all of the toys for me. Stretching motions, or quick movement could cause me to be in the hospital getting stitches again. I even had to get Zoe to help me put on and take off my shirts. It was embarrassing. So I'd told her I'd wear button downs so I wouldn't have to be so dependent.

Our search for those black dolls was challenging. We only found three in the whole store. Zoe complained to the manager about cultural awareness and that other races and ethnic groups needed some recognition. I don't ever think I've seen a grown man so intimidated. It was a sight to see. Forget about books with black women, we couldn't find any. We'd have to find those online and have them shipped to us.

"I'm going to write letters to these toy stores Anaya. And we are ordering some dolls that have afros and dreads! We'll throw in a few with some relaxed hair, but Nadia is going to see some naturalistas."

After the toy store we headed to Nadia's daycare. I turned off the car and told Zoe I'd go get Nadia. I wasn't quite sure I could pin down the smell of Nadia's daycare. It always smelt like a cross between crayons and cookies. The walls were blue and yellow, with paintings of children, letters, and numbers.

As I moved inside her classroom to the sign out sheet, Nadia raised her head and ran to me. "Auntie Naya!"

I smiled and leaned down to embrace her, as Nadia hugged my legs. I knew that her hugging my legs this tight might cause a bruise, but I savored her love. The feel of Nadia around my legs made me wonder how Julie could trade her daughter for a life of crime and sex. Although, I hadn't looked forward to having to raise Nadia on my own, it was better this way.

"Grab your bookbag, Nadia."

She ran to get it, her light-up sneakers sending pink lights glittering. She picked up her bookbag and came to me with it and I carefully bent to help her put it on her back and tighten the Velcro on her sneakers. By the time I rose up, I was thankful I'd avoided my skin ripping again.

I wanted to pick her up, but I couldn't risk it. I held her hand and she started walking with me. "So Nadia, I have a friend and her name is Zoe."

"Zoe?"

"Yes. But call her Auntie Zoe."

"That's a funny name."

I smiled. "Auntie Zoe is in the car so mi want you fi say hi and be nice. She's gonna be staying at our house fi a likkle while." I tried to speak in patois as much as possible to Nadia. It was the way Julie most likely spoke to her and I wanted her to learn the dialect.

She looked confused and then she started playing in her hair. "Does she like princess movies?"

"I'm sure she does. We actually bought you some dolls today. And we have some books we're getting for you too."

Nadia's eyes glittered with glee. "Yay!" she said, and hugged me tight around my neck. We got to the car and I looked at Zoe's face smiling when she saw Nadia and I. "There she is," I said to Nadia. "Don't forget to say hi and thank you for the dolls."

Nadia nodded and I opened the door of the car and put her in the car seat.

"Hi, Auntie Zoe!" Nadia chimed.

"Hi, Nadia!"

"Thank you for the dolls!"

"You're welcome sweetheart."

I finished strapping her in and moved to the driver's side. Zoe turned to me and rose her eyebrow. "So, I'm an aunt now."

"What can I say? I'm Jamaican, I'm not gonna have a three year old calling you by your first name like you two are the same age."

Zoe laughed. "You Jamaicans and your customs."

"Oh, you'll see way more. I try and make Nadia eat more traditional foods than the frozen food junk."

I reversed out the parking lot and drove. "I'm gonna tell you the same thing I told you in college. I don't eat goat," Zoe said.

"You will by the time you leave my house."

By the time we'd gotten home, I'd had to tear Nadia away from the dolls so that she could eat and after she had the freedom to play again, she spent the whole time jabbering to herself. She held the black baby doll, like she'd actually been skilled at holding a real child. She'd asked me tons of times when she'd be able to see Jeremy and I'd kept telling her soon. Every night, I'd lean over feeling this strangeness that Sean wasn't there. My milk hadn't completely dried up yet either. The first couple days that Sean had left, my breasts were so engorged that I cringed every time I remembered not wanting to breastfeed. Each time I'd have to put in the nursing pads, I'd have to fight back tears of guilt. I'd rejected my son. Zoe was playing with Nadia and pretending to be a pediatrician, although almost everything she was doing would in actuality be the wrong thing for a pediatrician to do.

"Auntie Naya."

"Yes, Nadi."

"Are you my mommy?"

I remembered what Julie said about treating Nadia like my own, but I didn't know whether I should tell her I was actually her mother or to tell her to keep calling me her aunt.

"No, sweetheart. Your mommy was my sister."

"Then where is she?"

She died was the logical answer. Not the answer you tell a three year old. At least I don't think you're supposed to tell that to a three year old. Zoe looked at me, her dark eyes piercing into mine. I came around to the rug Nadia and Zoe were sitting on.

"Nadia, your mother is in Jamaica. But, where she is we can't go right now."

Zoe made a face. Bad answer.

Nadia looked around and then her chin quivered. A sudden vision of Julie sitting across from me in the prison flashed across my mind. My chest felt tight and I looked to Zoe.

"Why not?" she started to wail.

"Your Auntie and I are here and we are gonna have so much fun. And soon your Uncle and your baby cousin will be here too. And they're more fun than us," Zoe said.

I shot Zoe a look. I didn't think we should be bringing Sean into this just yet.

"Everyone has a mommy but me." Nadia whimpered, heaving up sobs.

I put my hand to my mouth and tried to fight back my tears before I picked Nadia up. "I'm so sorry baby, I miss your mommy too. I really hope we can both see her soon." I rubbed my hand over her back, her small body still heaving. I gently put her head to rest on my shoulder. Zoe looked at me somberly, before getting up reaching for her purse and exiting. I didn't say anything to her, just sang "Mango Time" softly until Nadia quieted and fell asleep.

Thirty minutes later after I put Nadia down in her bed and sat at the kitchen table drinking cider in a wine glass Zoe walked in. She was still wearing her heels but at least she'd taken off the blazer she had on.

"Where have you been?" I asked.

"Important phone call."

I rose my eyebrows and went back to drinking. She walked over and picked up the bottle. "Grape cider?"

"Drinking is counterproductive. This is the

closest I can get to wine."

"Feeling that bad?"

I downed the glass and started to pour another. "Can you tell?"

"Where's the other wine glasses?" Zoe asked, kicking off her heels.

I pointed at the cupboard and she went and got herself one, rinsed it and poured herself a glass. "How's Nadia?"

"Asleep."

She drank some. "I remember back in college you used to tell me all the drama Julie used to get into. When did she pass?"

"Two years ago."

Zoe leaned back in her chair. "You're doing a great job."

"I'm scraping by. Next time, I think I'll just let her call me mommy. I think that's what Julie would have wanted."

Zoe nodded. "Whatever is best for her."

"I can barely hold her anymore. I don't know how long I'll be able to hold her." I really wanted to say *what if I die?* What if I had crossed over to the point of no return with this thing?

"That's why you have me," she said, taking another sip of the cider. Then she laughed. "This is really weird you know. I feel like I'm supposed to be drunk, but I'm drinking carbonated grape juice."

I laughed. "This is supposed to be a serious moment Zoe. I'm suffering."

That made her laugh even harder. "Why am I laughing so hard?"

"Maybe this stuff is stronger than we thought."

We both laughed and I downed the rest of my drink and made a show of sticking out my tongue and saying "ahh"! We were both silent for a little bit before I turned to her. "Thank you for being here. After all these years we still seem natural with each other. "

Zoe put down her glass. "I'm only doing for you what I know you would've done for me."

I smiled.

"How did it feel when you found out you had a melanoma?"

I rubbed my face. "I was terrified that it was going to travel to other places in my body. Just the thought of having cancer...." I shook my head. "It's different prescribing chemotherapy to your patients and watching them vomit and writhe in pain. As much as you feel for them, you still feel detached from it. It's different when it could possibly be you fighting for your life."

"When you get through this, you'll be a better doctor. You'll be a better person."

I nodded. "I wish Sean were here. I wish I could go back to the way things were before..." I stopped speaking and just looked ahead at the teething keychain on the kitchen counter that Jeremy would play with.

Zoe feigned offense. "I thought I was all you needed. I thought we were independent women." She finished her cider and then looked at me. "You could call him you know."

"I wouldn't really know how to begin. Plus, I don't want Sean coming back here just because he feels sorry for me because I'm sick."

Zoe rolled her eyes. "He's your husband. He vowed to be with you in sickness and in health."

"And he left me."

"You didn't really give him much choice, did you?"

"I didn't think he'd *actually* leave."

"And now your pride won't let you ask him to come back home."

I rolled my eyes.

"Pride goeth before destruction, and an haughty spirit before a fall."

"Since when did you start quoting the Bible?"

"Excuse you," she said, holding out her hand in front of my face. "I went to Sunday School too."

I ran my hand through my hair and leaned my head against the back of the chair. "Yeah, well I'll need you to pray for me and maybe read some scriptures when I have to go to the dermatologist in the morning."

"Will do, my sista," she said, laying her hand on my forehead. "I can't wait until your skin is nice and dark again."

I shot her a look.

"Anaya, I'm serious. Look at your face, your bone structure. You are a gorgeous woman. Do I need to put on India Arie?"

I giggled. "No, that won't be necessary."

"Tell me when was the first time you felt ugly."

"What kind of question is that?"

"A good one. Now answer it."

"You first."

Zoe's jaw tightened and she looked away for a moment. "Ok. My stepfather was the first to make me feel ugly."

"Your stepfather?" I asked and Zoe nodded. "You know I don't really know much about your family."

"There isn't a whole lot to tell. We're not much of a family."

"Well, that in itself is something to talk about Zo."

"Once upon a time," she said, in a grand gesture. "My mother met my father in college in Chicago. She was a sophomore pre-med student and he was a TA for chem lab. My mom said all the girls would wear their best outfits whenever he was teaching and make sure they had their push up bras. The girls were swooning over the TA with the butter colored skin. But, he seemed to not pay attention to them. He would always compliment my mother's work ethic and point out her accomplishments to the class. I guess mom started enjoying the attention and pretty soon she was returning his glances, welcoming his hand as it brushed over hers when he was showing her how to balance out an equations. You know all that romantic garbage," she said, waving her hand in dismissal.

"She told me she slept with him three times," she said, holding up three fingers for me to see. "It's probably more. Mothers don't want to admit the truth about their sex life to their daughters," we both smirked at that.

"Two weeks before her final exams, mom found out he was married, when he'd left his wallet accidently in her apartment. There was a picture of him with his wife and son. When she confronted him, he'd only reminded her that they agreed to an affair and she shouldn't be upset. She broke things off with him, finished the semester and one month later rushed into the drugstore after she realized her period was late. She said she must've peed on about five of those things and they were all positive. Mom went back home, transferred to a local college and lived at home with my grandparents."

"Did your mother tell your father about you?" I asked.

Zoe shook her head. "No. Her stubbornness and independence never let her go back and tell him that he had a child. As far as she was concerned she didn't want or need his help and she doubted he wanted to give her any help either. He had a family. My mother decided she would make her own. But she didn't. She was *always* working, and when she wasn't working, she was doing something for herself. My mom has only been there to write a check for me."

I ran my finger along the rim of my glass. "Did you ever try to find him?"

"No, when I was kid I wondered about him a lot,

but then after some time I just began to resent him."

"Because he had a family without you?"

"No, I mean he didn't know about me, and it wasn't like I was poor and he had money, I resented him because he was the reason I was so light."

"What? You hated him for making you look like a model?"

Zoe rolled her eyes and shook her head. "It's not like that. I don't look like my mother or any of my family for that matter. I look like him. And I felt like an outsider because of it. My mom's family kinda always made me feel like I was special because of my skin. But, something about their 'love' for me felt... wrong."

I made a face and she tried to clarify. "They'd tell me things like girl, don't you ever be like your cousins and play in the sun all day and ruin your complexion. Or, better yet, 'you don't need to read all those books, just be a model Zoe. Who needs brains when you've got looks?'"

I looked down. "So, what happened to make you hate your skin? Girls work hard to have your skin, your hair. You're a rapper's dream," I said.

Zoe smirked. "Humans always want what they don't have."

I ran my hand through my hair. She continued, "My mom went to school when I was a toddler. She didn't want to give up on her dream of becoming a doctor and grandma and grandpa wouldn't let her either. When she graduated from med school I was almost seven years old. We moved out of my grandparents' house to a small apartment close by the hospital where she was doing her residency. She met my stepfather there." She sighed and rolled her eyes, "I always hated him."

"He was the first to call me light bright. Light Bright, damn near white. And mom just sat there and giggled because *everything* that he said was just *so clever*." She gave a sardonic smile. "He was one of those 'intellectual types', *always* studying some ancient history book. Mom married him when I was 10, and I just attempted to stay out of his way as much as possible."

"He was that horrible?" I asked.

"He was just irritating. He took every opportunity to put me down. Called me a house nigger. I didn't even understand what that really meant until I got to high school. And then, school wasn't much better."

"People teased you at school?"

"Some did. Boys liked me. I won't lie. But that created problems. I was quiet and introverted and the girls were…. Sorry to say this, but, jealous. When I wasn't reading, I was running home to keep from getting into fights with the other girls at school. I was always too stuck up, my hair too nice. When I was 13, I didn't get away and before getting my face punched a couple times, I got some Nair lathered on my head. By the time I had gotten home, I had to be taken to the barber to shave off everything."

"So you know what it's like to be bald?"

"Yes, girl."

"So after that you wanted to change your looks."

"Bingo. I stopped relaxing my hair, because it made people mistake me for a white girl or a Latina. I was determined to not stay in the house, I was gonna stay outside and darken my skin by any means necessary. That was hard to do in Chicago. So by the time I was 15, I was already a regular at the tanning salon. I didn't care about all the warnings about the risks involved." Regret seemed stamped on her forehead. "But for the first time my stepfather liked the way I looked. At least it was caramel and not that God-awful white man's skin he said. I told him that my father wasn't white. He just would roll his eyes and say 'close enough'".

I looked down. "I didn't think that-"

"That light-skinned people have problems too?" she asked, raising an eyebrow and smiling.

"I just thought you all would have less to worry about in that area. I mean you could've passed if-"

She shook her head. "The idea of passing to me is disgusting. I could never do that and have peace." She tapped her finger on her glass. "If I passed, I would've reinforced this idea that something was wrong me, with being black and that being something else was better."

"But in this world, it *is* better to be something

else."

"Well, then the world is wrong. I shouldn't have to conform to what it tells me."

I understood. "We say that in church you know."

Zoe smiled. "Yeah, they do say that in church. Guess it never made sense until now."

"Yeah, and what you said never made sense to me until now."

She smiled and then sighed. "We're both endangering our lives to be on the opposite end of the 'color spectrum'."

I bit my lip. "Kinda seems stupid now."

"Yeah, it does." She sipped at her drink.

"I was six. The first time I felt ugly. I was six."

Zoe nodded and we both stayed silent for a long time.

I looked over at the clock on the nightstand. 1:06 am. The sheets still held the smell of Sean's cologne and most of his clothes still remained. Sometimes I'd come home and realize he'd been here while I was gone to collect more clothes or stuff for Jeremy. I sighed and rose up from the bed. What if I never got to the point where reconciliation could happen? My child would grow up feeling motherless.

Our room faced the back of the house with the pool. I opened the sliding door that led to the poolside. I hadn't been in the pool in awhile. Especially not when I had those stiches. Going in the pool might not even be good with a damaged epidermis. All that chlorine has better access into my skin, now that at least two out of four of the layers of my epidermis are damaged...all that medical knowledge and no common sense to stop what I was doing before it got to this point.

I hiked my long silky nightgown and sat down, sinking my feet into the water. One time my mother had gotten the flu, the only time I remember seeing her sick. She didn't even want to get out of bed so my dad took my sister and I to town to get some new school clothes. Roy had stayed behind with my mother to help her. As we got in his old Volvo we listened to the sounds of Beres Hammond singing, "Love Means Never to Say You're Sorry"

Julie asked, "Daddy, how do you know somebody loves you?"

Daddy looked at Julie. She always asked the questions I was too afraid to ask. He answered her, "When they see you at your worst and still love you."

"So you mean when dem see you wid rollers, and nose snot?"

He laughed that big laugh that always seemed too big for his small frame. "Yeah, when dem see di ugliness on the outside, but more when dem see di ugliness on the inside and still love you."

I had said "oh" that day, but I never understood what my father meant until now. I used my arms to push myself into the water. I floated along the pool, humming. The sound vibrated in my ears. Beres and the writers of *Love Story* missed something in my opinion. Love meant that I *had* to say sorry.

I started to backstroke in the water, not thinking of my fragile skin, only of Sean and Jeremy. Was Sean managing everything on his own? Jordan was Jeremy's godfather, but Jordan knew nothing about taking care of babies, he probably wouldn't be much help to Sean. I thought of my son growing up to be like his father, self-assured and confidant. How did that happen? How did some of us grow up grasping for validation, while others cruised on by calling themselves African kings and queens in a world that has taught us we are anything but royalty?

Sean had given this presentation for his university a month ago during Black History Month on black beauty. The students had loved him and I sat there oblivious to what he was truly saying even though he'd looked me right in the eye. "Black beauty doesn't lie in the relative darkness or lightness of one's skin. In the silkiness, curliness, or kinkiness of one's hair. It lies in the resilience of the spirit, in the kindness of the soul. Black beauty isn't what you look like, it's what you are."

5 REMEDIES

The phone rang at 7:00 am. I looked at the caller ID and saw that it was a number from Jamaica. Mum. Only she called at the break of dawn. I picked up.

"Mum."

"Good evening."

I smiled. "How are you?"

"Good. It's been nice and cool. How's Nadia?"

My mother and father had been the only ones I'd told about Nadia.

"She's doing well, she's energetic. She loves to sing and learn."

"Your father has been asking when your

family will come and visit," my mom said.

"Soon, Mum. We will come soon."

"You sound tired. How are you?"

I wasn't sure whether I should lie or not. Roy and Julie fed her enough lies to last a lifetime. "I'm not doing so well."

"Why what happened?"

I drew in a breath, uncertain how to properly say it. "Sean left."

"What?! Mi need fi call him. Yuh just have baby! He-"

"It's not his fault."

She was silent for a while and then she spoke. "What happened?"

"I was just terrible Mum. He left and he took Jeremy with him."

"He took *your* baby with him?"

Jeremy is technically ours, not just mine. "He needed to. Mum, I... there are things about me that you don't know. When I moved to Kingston, I was trying so hard to make my way and to be someone important...I, um, I started bleaching."

"Bleaching?" she asked roughly.

"Yes," I said, feeling chastised. "I don't know, I just thought I'd look nicer if I looked different, if my skin was lighter. So I bleached and I kept doing it and Sean didn't like it." I started to cry. "I treated my son like he was trash, because I thought he was too dark, and I made life hell for Sean. I don't deserve for them to be here. For them to put up with this. I'm very sick now. My skin it's very fragile. It will tear, bruise... I have to be seeing doctors to make sure I don't have cancer."

I heard her release a breath. "Anaya, why would you do all of this to yourself? You were my most beautiful daughter."

"No, I wasn't. Julie was. You always said so."

"I never said that."

"Yes, you did. I remember when I was six and those boys teased me about how black I was. I came home, and you told me I was black and there was nothing I could do about it, so I just had to deal with it. I didn't want to deal with it when I got older. I thought I had a way out."

"And this was a good way out?" she asked me.

I stayed silent.

"Anaya, your memory is failing you. You came home that day and you were crying. And you know I have never taught you to pity yourself. So, I said, 'Roses don't fight over what color they are. They accept their colors and bloom. And each of them are beautiful.'"

I wiped tears from my face. "I don't remember that part."

"We often remember the things we want to hear, not always the things we need to hear."

"I don't know what to do."

"You know what you need to do. My son in law and grandson needs to be back in that house and when you come back home, your skin needs to be fine."

I smiled. Mum, always giving out orders. "Yes, Ma'am. Do you have any remedies I can take?"

"In the morning drink some Bizzy tea and clean out that poison. Then drink a cup cerassee everyday."

"God, Mummy, Cerassee is nasty-"

She silenced me. "Listen to me."

"Ok. Cerassee and what else?"

"Aloe Vera. Do all of that and I promise in a while you'll begin to look and feel like yourself."

I nodded. "Thank you," I whispered.

"Don't thank me. I need to pray for you and your household. That's why I can't live in America....too many problems you people have."

I laughed. I love my mother.

The morning was a blur. I could barely remember getting Nadia ready for school. I also had to put Zoe on her emergency contact card. For the first time, the smell of cookies and crayons made me feel sick. I scribbled Zoe's name on the contact list and Sean's name. Sean. I'm going to get a follow up at the dermatologist and Sean isn't going to be there. The man I used to tell everything to. Everything except my deepest fears and hurts. The sides of ourselves that most people hide during the early stages of the dating process, but eventually come clean about. No, I wanted to seem perfect. I wanted to be perfect in front of my husband, my colleagues, even in front of God. I touched my phone and started to dial his number, but then erased it each time. What was I supposed to say, "Hey Sean I'm getting treatment for melanoma. My skin rips and bruises if I roll over too fast in bed." Yeah, I didn't perceive that going over well.

Before he left, we went to church every week and each time I sat there thinking the pastor had to be talking to some really messed up people. Not to me.

People text and call all the time to see if everything is alright and why I haven't been in church, but I lie. I say it's work or the flu. No, I don't need chicken noodle soup. Hmph. What I need is a slap in the head, some tonic, my husband, and Jesus. Not necessarily in that order.

It's funny how I'd always thought Jesus had made a mistake with how he'd made me and now I was begging for me to return the way I was, just so I wouldn't have to deal with all of this.

Zoe drove me to the dermatologist. I already knew my dermatologist would be horrified like he was the last time, but I prayed that we would at least give me some hope.

Dr. Trujillo was a colleague of mine, and now my physician. I'd had him swear not to tell anyone this right now. If any other physicians heard about this, I wanted them to hear this from me. But I couldn't tell them now. At least not yet. How would I explain to them that I warned patients everyday not to do the things I had done to myself? Thankfully, his office looked more like a spa than a doctor's office, so most would think I was just here for something cosmetic. I'd taken a six-month leave from work, pretending it was an extended vacation from my maternity leave.

I was escorted to a room and told the doctor would be with me shortly. I rested back against the procedure chair.

"You ok?" Zoe asked.

I nodded. "Just a little scared." I scratched at one of the scars from where the stitches had been removed. I had seven of them. Two from when my skin on both of my arms ripped, the others were from the melanomas that were removed. Two on my stomach, one on my hip, one on the back of my hand, and the major one was on my neck. My doctor was more concerned about the one on my neck, considering it could spread to my lymph nodes. Thankfully, that hadn't happened.

Zoe came over to my bedside. "Remember last night when you said you wished Sean was with you?"

"Yes," I said, suspiciously.

"Well, he should be here any moment."

"I told you not to tell him."

"And I didn't tell him you had paper skin or melanomas. I told him you might need his support and that you had a dermatologist appointment and then I texted him the address."

I glared at her.

"I should probably let you know that I told him about Nadia too. He was pretty excited about that. Not too excited that you kept it from him though, but

I'm pretty sure you two can work that out."

I sighed. "I'm gonna get you back for this."

She pursed her lips. "I know darling, you can just thank me later."

I rested back against the chair and closed my eyes. "I'm going to use the bathroom," Zoe said. I didn't open my eyes and waved goodbye at her. I heard the door open and opened my eyes expecting to see Dr. Trujillo. It was Sean. I sat up and didn't say anything. He came over and rested his hand on my hair. "It's alright," he said, soothingly and I looked up at him.

Zoe walked back inside and gave an innocent grin. "Oops, that was fast, well, it looks like I can leave and get some grocery shopping done."

"Zoe," I said.

"Don't worry Naya, I will pick up Nadia from school and everything. I'll surprise her and take her somewhere fun. Just let me know when's a good time to bring her home. I won't feed her any junk food or let her watch horror movies."

I motioned for her to come close. She made a

face. "You know it might make you look bad to threaten me in front of your husband, especially if he files divorce papers. I mean what would the judge think?"

I narrowed my eyes. "I hate you."

"I love you too, Naya," she said, gathering her things. "Sean, I know you'll take really good care of your wife."

Sean chuckled. "I will," he said, looking at me.

Zoe came over to my bedside and whispered, "You did good. He's cute and the smart, sensitive type."

I narrowed my eyes and she winced. "Oh, I'm sensing a lot of hostility. You know what, I'll see you when you're in a better mood. Sean, please keep me updated if she doesn't return my calls or texts."

"No problem," he said, and Zoe winked at me before she left.

Sean rubbed his thumb over my hand, running his hand along the fresh scar. He didn't ask.

I finally met his eyes. "Aren't you the slightest mad at me for not telling you?"

"Yeah, I am, but I don't think yelling and arguing will make the situation better right now."

Dr. Trujillo walked in then. "Hello." He stopped and held out his hand, "Dr. Blake?"

"Yes," Sean and I said. I smiled inwardly, whenever someone said Dr. Blake, neither of us was sure which one of us, the person was referring to.

Dr. Trujillo laughed. "I meant this Dr. Blake," he said, shaking Sean's hand. "I'm so glad you were able to make it to this appointment."

"Me too," Sean said. I knew I would have to give an explanation later.

Dr. Trujillo began to examine all my stitches. "These look like they're healing nicely. He looked at the ones on my arms. He wasn't the one who stitched those. I got those done at the ER.

"My skin tore."

I felt Sean's eyes on me and Dr. Trujillo nodded. "How much difficulty do you have with the tearing?" he asked.

Sean's presence was distracting me. I felt hot. I felt shame. "Um... I can do most things. I can't stretch or lift heavy items."

"Ok. So are the topical creams gone?"

Not exactly. "I don't use them anymore." *That was the truth.*

He looked at me to verify if I was telling the truth. "Good. Ok, well, it looks like everything is healing nicely. But, remember I still think that maybe you should see someone in psych about this Dr. Blake."

"And like I said before, I'll think about it."

"There's nothing wrong with mental health. As a physician I thought you believed in that."

"I do," I said. "But, I don't have a mental illness. I just need to start believing the truth and not lies. It's simple. I don't mind going somewhere I can just talk through it. However, to be possibly put on medication is not something for me."

He nodded again. "I understand." He jotted some things down on his notepad and let me know that he would see me again in six weeks. He exited the room.

I rubbed at my temples. "I feel a bit

overwhelmed."

"Come on. Let's go," Sean said. We exited the office and started walking towards his truck. I got in and fastened my seatbelt. He got in and did the same and pulled off. I looked out the window and tapped my nail against my teeth.

"So what excuse have you been using to explain why I'm not around?"

"Just that you're working or busy. What excuse have you been using about me?"

"Same."

I smiled.

"How is it staying with Jordan? How is he? Where's Jeremy?"

"Wow that's a lot of questions," he turned onto US 1. "Jordan is good, working on some top secret album production. He won't even tell me who the artist is. But he's wrapping up now. Staying with him feels like...college." He laughed. "Jeremy is with Jordan."

I opened my mouth in protest.

"He's fine. I promise. Jordan has gotten a lot

better with babies. Jeremy will survive."

I wanted to yell at him for leaving the baby with Jordan, for not bringing him here to see me, but instead I bit down on my bottom lip and felt the burn of tears. Sean looked over at me and moved his hand towards me and then drew back.

"I'm so sorry. I'm sorry for Jeremy and for doing this to myself. I'm sorry for not telling you about Nadia. I'm sorry for being messed up."

He just stared and didn't say anything.

"I know what I'm saying won't make it all better. I understand you'll probably still want a divorce or to take custody of Jeremy. I won't fight you. I-"

"I miss you."

"What?"

"I'm not filing for divorce. I'm not filing for custody of Jeremy."

"Why not?"

He gave a small smile.

"You love me," I said. Daddy was right.

Sean nodded. "But, I want you to work on yourself Naya."

I nodded. "Whatever it will take. I'll do it."

Sean nodded again. "Tell me about the new addition to our family," he said, changing the subject.

I played with the handle of my purse on my lap. "Her name is Nadia. My niece. She's so cute, Sean. I love her already."

"I want to meet her."

"I want you to meet her too. We can take her to the park and the beach and maybe even to Disney World. She'd love Magic Kingdom. She'd get to meet all the princesses. She's obsessed with them."

"Let's get you back to good health and then we can talk about all those trips."

"Ok, and when you meet her she'll just want to watch TV, or sing, or dance, play dolls and have tea parties. She reminds me of Julie so much and I think that's what scares me."

"She won't make the same mistakes."

"How do you know?"

"We'll raise her differently."

"My parents loved us and Julie and Roy still made their choices. I don't think you can predict your kids' futures. You can only pray for them."

"Then we'll pray."

"I haven't been to church since you left."

"I know."

I raised my eyebrows.

"Cause I've been going," he said.

"Have you been praying for me?"

"Yes."

"Good, cause I've been praying too."

He changed the subject. "What does she look like?"

I smiled. "I think she looks like me."

Sean smiled back. "Then I know she's beautiful."

For the first time I believed him when he said it.

6 ALONE TIME

Sean pulled up to our house and I got out. He got out of the car.

"You're coming inside?"

"What am I not welcome inside my own home?"

"No..." He looked shocked. "I mean yes, you can come. I just didn't think you'd want to."

"No, I'm ready to come home and spend some time with my wife."

I smiled shyly. "Ok."

I have a good husband. A very good one. Fifty... ok seventy five percent of our arguments stemmed from dumb things I'd do or from my internal problems. Still he'd stuck by me. Even though my job can be demanding he's always been there for me. Sean would massage my feet after a long day and let me sleep in and bring breakfast to me. Sometimes Jordan teased him that he was whipped, but we all knew that wasn't necessarily true. It wasn't like I bossed him around or anything. He does these things...just because. Because he loves me. Man, I'm an idiot.

I do nice things for Sean too. Well, I did nice things for him on his birthday, like the time I got him courtside tickets to the Heat game. I did nice things on our anniversary and Christmas. Occasions. I guess maybe that wasn't all that great considering he did stuff for me year round. Again, I'm an idiot.

I opened the door to the house and stepped inside.

"Clean. As always," he said behind me.

"I make Nadia pick up all her toys once she's done playing. Let me show you her room."

I turned around and noticed that Sean was looking back at me.

"What?"

"Nothing. I'm just taking it all in."

I turned and started walking. I could feel him following behind.

"This is it." I said leading him into her room with her pink and purple comforter and barbies all stuffed into a corner.

"I take it she likes dolls," he said amused.

"Correction. She *loves* dolls."

"Oh, man." He reached over and picked up one with an afro. "You got these for her?"

"Zoe thought it was important for her to have a variety of dolls with different shades and ethnicities."

He laughed. "Good." We both looked at each other for a while. "You look pretty, I mean the way the light is hitting you right now.' I looked to my left and noticed the light coming through the window.

"Pretty, is a bit of a strong word."

"No, it's a mild one."

I fumbled with my hands and took a deep breath. "I'm messing this up. Can you say it again?"

"What?"

"Say what you just said again."

"You look pretty. No, you look beautiful."

I looked back at him and nodded. "Thank you."

He smirked. "I'm not convinced."

"What did I do wrong?"

He walked past me and made his way into our bedroom. I followed him.

"You gotta at least say it with some conviction."

He stood up crossed his arms over his chest, waiting for an answer. He was wearing a pullover Temple University sweater, a pair of jeans and some sneakers.

"Do you remember all the times you would tell me I was beautiful?"

His brow furrowed. "I'm not sure if you expect me to remember *each* time I said it."

I smiled. "No, I guess I'm thinking aloud. I never said anything back whenever you'd say it. Didn't you ever wonder why?"

"Yeah. I just assumed that maybe you already knew you were."

"And then after a while you realized I didn't."

He nodded.

I played with my fingers. "I haven't been loving you or Jeremy because I don't even know how to love myself."

Sean sat down on the bed. I sat down next to him. "What would make you love yourself Anaya?"

"I don't know. I'm not sure."

"What don't you love about yourself?"

"You already know some of it."

"No, I want you to tell me. I want you to say it aloud." He looked ahead out of our sliding glass door at the pool.

I sat up stiffly. "I don't love my..." I cleared my throat. "I don't love my..." I sighed. "Sean this is dumb."

"You know I used to think it was dumb until my wife started acting psychotically jealous and smearing chemicals all over her body." That stung a bit. Actually that stung a lot. Psychotically jealous? Was I really that bad?

"I'd realized you'd actually lost it when you told

me to have an affair. Oh, not just any affair, one with a white woman." Thank God he didn't bring up Jeremy.

"I said that?"

"Yeah, you said that. Not sure if you were daring me to really do it."

"I guess I thought if you did, it would justify the way I felt about myself. That I wasn't as good as another person."

"That's why I wouldn't give you the satisfaction."

I smirked. Oh, but I bet he thought about it. Probably thought about it long and hard, too. I couldn't even be mad. I mean I had told him to do it.

"Ok, so answer the question already. What don't you love about yourself?" he asked.

"I just think I'm plain. There's nothing special or beautiful about me." My eyes were misting. But I sat back refusing to cry. The pathetic thing is I'm not crying over having the most fragile skin and melanomas, I'm crying over being dark. I'm twisted.

Sean's eyes pierced mine. "What do you wish

was different about you?"

I rolled my eyes.

"Ok, let's start with your eyes. Would you want them to be different or would you keep them the same?"

"I would change them."

"And what would they look like?"

I shrugged. "I don't know anything besides this plain brown."

He got up and walked over to my dresser. He opened the drawer and pulled out the creams I kept stored. How he'd known they were right there, I don't know. "You know your eyes remind me of coffee beans?" he said, as he squeezed one of the creams out the tube and straight into the garbage.

"Coffee beans?" I said, my voice not hiding my annoyance.

"Yes," he said, leaning down and kissing each of my eyes. "You know how much I love coffee," he whispered.

"And you know how much I hate it," I whispered back.

"They're still real pretty. Even now. And the shape of them, Anaya." He said, as he took another jar out and read the label before scooping all the contents into the trash. "I wish you could see how they change color sometimes and the way they glitter when you're happy or get real dark when you're mad."

"They do that?"

"Uh huh. You don't get to catch that in the mirror."

"What color are they now?" I asked, challenging him.

He only smirked and squeezed another tube into the garbage.

I looked back up at Sean, at his brown eyes. "Yours remind me of tamarind balls."

He laughed. "You mean those sweetly sour things you brought home one time."

I grinned. "Yeah."

"I'm guessing that's a compliment."

I nodded.

"Giving out compliments at a time like this?" He

ran a thumb over my lips. "Please don't tell me you'd change these."

"No, those can stay the same."

"Are you giving yourself a compliment?"

"I think I am."

He smiled and leaned down and kissed my lips. The sweetness of the gesture filled me. His hand rested on my hair.

"Well, you women do so much to your hair I'm not even sure you can judge it right now. What does your natural hair look like?"

I sighed and leaned back. "It used to be so poofy and soft and my mother used to spend the whole afternoon combing and braiding our hair."

"Hmm. Maybe I'll get to enjoy that poofiness soon."

"We'll see. I'm not sure if I'm ready for all of that. But, I'll consider stopping the keratin treatments."

He kissed my head. "You'll be beautiful still. And I look forward to seeing all that poofiness in its glory."

"I know you don't want to change your body. I see you all the time feelin' yourself."

"Lef mi alone." I said, playfully.

"Iz true," he said, imitating my accent.

He touched the skin on my arms. "Your skin is still soft."

I stiffened and he looked up into my eyes.

"When I first met you, your skin reminded me of chocolate."

"What kind of chocolate?"

He gave a faint smile. "Godiva."

"Milk or dark?"

"Dark."

I looked away at that. "What does it look like now?"

"Like a ghost of what it once was."

"Does it look like Godiva chocolate anymore at all?"

"Not any I've seen."

I ran my hand along his jaw. "If I knew back then what I knew now, I would say, no I wouldn't change a thing."

Sean kissed my hand. "Your color will come back, we just have to take care of ourselves, right?"

I nodded and he kissed his way up my arm and then kissed my lips again. "Do you want to go for a swim?"

"If you're up it."

I kissed him again giving him my answer.

"I'll go get some towels and take out this trash," he said, lifting the trashcan with all the creams out of the room. "Meet me at the pool."

7 WE ARE FAMILY

Evidently Sean and Zoe had set up for the day to be interruption free. Nadia had ended up spending the night at Zoe's house. Sean was out in the kitchen making breakfast. I sat up in bed and dialed Zoe.

"Hello."

"Hey Zo."

"Oh, hey you. You sound pretty chipper. How was the first night?"

"Great."

There was silence on the other end of the phone.

"Zoe?"

"I'm here," she said, and I played with the sheets. "You and Sean kissed and made up I see."

"What would make you think that?"

"Because you sound like a woman who's had a *great* night. You were always the one in college saying you should never kiss on the first date and with Sean you always throw away the rulebook."

"He's my husband! I can kiss him anytime I want!" I said, laughing.

She tisked her tongue. "Well, while you were getting your groove back, I was with Nadia having a grand ol' time. We read books, listened to music-

"What kind of music?"

"TLC."

"What?!"

"Yeah. TLC, No Scrubs."

"I told you to have her do *educational* things."

"This *is educational*. When one of them little boys steps to her on the playground now she knows what to do."

I shook my head. "You are something else."

"You should hear her though. She had her hands on her hips and she was shaking her finger while she was singing the song. Girl, I'm gonna have her sing it for you when she comes by later."

I laughed. "Keep those songs G rated, Zoe."

"If G means gangsta, gully, or goon, then we're good."

I sighed loudly.

"I'm just kidding. I had the clean version. She'll be fine. I won't ruin her innocence of mind until I have *the talk* with her when she's ten."

"Goodness."

"You're the one that announced that I'm Auntie Zoe. Aunties get special privileges."

I chuckled. "Well, I'm glad she's enjoying you and you're enjoying her."

"Yes, makes me think about having some little chicks as soon as I can actually get a man."

I giggled and Sean walked through the door with breakfast.

"Ok, Zo, I'll see you later. Bring Nadia after

school."

"Oh, I see. Your husband is back in the room. Tell him I said hi and to behave himself."

"Zoe said hi," I said to Sean.

"And that he's naughty," she said over the phone.

"Bye Zo," I said, giggling as I hung up.

"Was that a session of 'girl talk'?" Sean asked, handing me a cup of tea.

"You can say that." I said, blowing on the tea to cool it.

"I'm glad you have a 'girl friend' again," he said, giving air quotes. "What happened between you two?"

"I'm not even sure we can answer that. *Life* happened and we drifted apart for a while. And when everything started to cave in, other than you, she was the only person I could think of talking to."

He nodded. "Your friend Zoe can be *very* persuasive."

"She's a lawyer. She gets paid to be persuasive."

He laughed and started drinking his coffee.

"I invited her to stay with me and help me with Nadia. I had no idea that she was going to call you... what did she say to you?"

He scooped up some the scrambled eggs with a fork and put the fork close to my mouth. "You need something in your stomach." I took it from him and ate.

"Well, she called me and told me that she was a college friend of yours and that you'd contacted her because you were sick and possibly in need of a lawyer."

"Zoe handles family law, so I figured you'd contacted her either for a divorce or about adoption after she told me about Nadia."

"She is handling the adoption process with Nadia. I came to her initially about a divorce. I thought you might file one, since I hadn't heard from you in a while."

He sighed. "I should've called. But, every time I reached for the phone I'd get mad all over again."

I swallowed. "I wasn't what you signed up for. All my issues."

"No, they weren't, but I made a vow and I intend on keeping it."

"Thank you," I said, quietly munching on some of the French toast. "So what did Zoe tell you about my sickness?"

"She wouldn't tell me exactly what your sickness was, but when she told me to meet her at the dermatologist, I had a pretty big clue. The doctor confirmed what I didn't know."

"I know you want to say I told you so about those creams."

"No, I want to say I wish you would've realized you didn't need them sooner. But, it's too late for all of that. We're here and we're going to make it through this together."

"You were really serious about those vows, huh?"

"Yes, ma'am. In sickness and in health, in craziness and in sanity."

I laughed. "I don't remember that one."

"Well, I'm adding that."

"Thank you for throwing out those creams

yesterday. I know that needed to happen. Now I can heal my body."

He kissed my cheek. "First your soul and then your body."

"I don't know how to solve the problem in the soul."

"Neither do I, but God does, and I think that once that one is gone perhaps the one in your body will be fixed faster."

"Should I get a counselor, go on a self discovery journey in Africa? Sean, I just don't know."

He laughed. "Self-discovery journey in Africa? Anaya, you can be so funny. I mean, hey, Africa is beautiful, I showed you the pictures of me all over the continent. But, you can find yourself here in North America, here in Miami."

I sighed and looked out the window at the palm trees planted in different spots along the parking lot. "You're right."

"You also should've known you could call me and tell me about all of this, about Nadia too."

"Pride. I didn't want to admit I'd messed up, and

that you were right. Then with Nadia, I guess I was surprised by the irony of it all. Me being a bad mom and then my sister pretty much drops her kid off permanently with me, a little girl who looks like she's mine."

He laughed and then stuffed some of the muffin in his mouth. "I'm telling you, it was fate."

He dusted off his hands and looked out the window. "Never thought we'd even be having this conversation. Four years of marriage, four years of me trying to convince you that you're beautiful. I think I'm slightly bitter that Zoe spends two days with you and you've changed your mind."

"I'm not so sure it was Zoe that changed my mind."

"Then what did?"

"Didn't you say you've been praying?"

"True that."

"I guess what hit me was the reality of what I'd done and how stupid it was. Then meeting Nadia and seeing how beautiful she is. How could I look at her and see her beauty and not see mine? Then I thought about Jeremy..." I choked on my tears. "I thought about him and how I didn't want to breastfeed him and how I looked at him with this...disgust. It wasn't a disgust for him as much as it was disgust for myself. I feel...terrible. I wish I could hold him again and tell him I'm sorry even though he doesn't understand." I wiped at my nose. "I want to be a good mother."

Sean gazed at me. "Do you know what your name means?"

"No... My mom just came up with it I guess."

"You should look it up, it means freedom."

"Seriously?"

He nodded. "And this is the freest I've ever seen you."

Sean and I spent the rest of the day in bed, before we finally dragged ourselves out to the store to get all the herbs my mother told me I needed. Sean used to laugh at all my natural remedies for everything. But, eventually he had to acknowledge that it worked and with far less side effects.

In the evening, I sat down on the couch watching TV when I heard the door open and Nadia's voice.

"Auntie Naya!"

I looked over and grinned as Nadia rushed into the room, ready to try to jump on me before Zoe said, "Whoa, pumpkin."

"Hey, Nadi, how are you?"

"I'm good."

"Come give me a kiss."

Zoe lifted her onto the couch and Nadia held my face and gave me a big kiss on my cheek.

"Did you have fun with Auntie Zoe?"

Nadia smiled and nodded her head, her eyes glittering. I noticed then her new hairdo; her hair twisted along the front and then let out in a big poof in the back, instead of how I would normally pull her hair back out of her face.

"I like your hair," I said, touching it. "Zo, you did this?"

"Uh huh. And just as promised, Nadia let's show Auntie Naya your dance moves."

Nadia blushed.

"Come on. I wanna see," I said.

"I'll do it with you," Zoe said, and Nadia scurried off the couch.

I watched as Zoe sang the chorus of "No Scrubs" while they both danced, shaking their fingers and adding actions to all the words. Sean's deep laugh came next and Zoe and Nadia turned for the first time noticing him.

"Oh, hey Sean. So sorry, I didn't see you over there." Zoe looked embarrassed. I smirked.

"Hey Zoe. I see you two have been having fun."

Nadia looked shy and hugged onto Zoe's legs.

"Nadia, that's your Uncle Sean. Say hi."

"Hi," she said, shyly before running over to me, and tapping me on my side. She crawled onto the couch and scooted close to me, burying herself in the crook of my arm.

"Auntie," she said, tapping me.

"Yes."

"He's my Uncle?"

"Yes."

"Not my Daddy?"

"No, but you can call him that if you want. You can call me mommy if you want to."

Nadia looked at me and thought for a little, while playing with my face.

"Ok."

"Ok what? You want to call me mommy?"

She nodded.

"And you want him to be your Daddy?" I whispered to her.

She nodded and buried her head in my shoulder.

"Ok, well ask him."

"Can you ask him?"

I looked into her coffee bean eyes and then back at Sean. "Nadia would like to know if she can call you Daddy."

Sean's face was serious. "Did she really ask that?"

I smiled and nodded.

He got up and walked over to us and I saw Zoe smile and then take a seat in the chair by the wall. He looked down at Nadia. "I'd love to be your Daddy."

Nadia smiled shyly at him she looked back at me. "Say thank you and give him a hug."

And before I knew it, she was in his arms. I think it was the best moment of my life.

8 IDEOLOGIES

I woke up to the sun peeking out at me. After that day Nadia and Sean had met, Zoe had gone back to her home even though I'd asked her to stay. She didn't want to intrude. But, I'd given her a key and told her to still come by and help me out on the days Sean had to be at work. Jeremy had come home and I savored every moment with him, even if it meant no sleep. I held him every chance I got, inhaled his scent, kissed him and played with his hands and feet. Last night, I'd barely gotten any rest because I'd gotten him so excited that he'd barely slept. I looked over at the clock and saw that it was already 10 am.

Nadia was supposed to go to school already. I got out of bed when I saw the note on my dresser.

Took Nadia to school and Jeremy out to the park. Wanted you to get some rest. Be back by 11. --- Zoe.

I smiled and sighed. God bless Zoe. I took a shower, brushed my teeth, made my way to the kitchen and began to boil some of the cerassee. Mum was right, already my body felt better and my skin glowed. I sat on the couch watching Phineas and Ferb, one of Nadia and Jeremy's favorites when Zoe walked through the door holding Jeremy. She handed him to me and he giggled and drooled on me as I kissed him good morning.

"Thank you so much."

"You looked like you needed it. You slept through all the noise this morning."

I smiled. "I never did ask, how many days did you take off from work?"

"Well, since I haven't taken a vacation and only one sick day in three years. I took a month off." For once Zoe didn't look like she was off to work. She wore a v-neck burgundy shirt with some jeans and sandals.

"A month?!"

"I need it. I need the rest."

"Rest? You're taking care of two children."

"I'm also taking care of that Jordan guy. He's a trip. When I had to go over there the first time to pick up Jeremy. I mean he does well with the baby, but you know Jeremy needs a woman's touch. He needs his mama. That boy has grabbed me so many times thinking he's gonna get milk."

I laughed. "Once I get back on my feet, you need to take a vacation."

"Once you get in tip top shape, I'll be lonely."

I held her hand. "Nope, cause I'll still need you to help me out during the day."

"Just as long as I don't intrude on your husband."

"You won't be."

"I want you two to bond with each other again and bond as a family with Jeremy and Nadia. You'll need some time. Plus, you need to get back to work

Doc, or did you forget you're a doctor?"

"I will. When I'm ready. But, promise me you won't lose contact. You can still come everyday if you want. We both have things to work through."

"I promise you won't get rid of me this time." Zoe smiled and looked at the television that was still running. "Sean and Nadia are so cute together. I nearly cry whenever I see them."

"He's gonna spoil that child. He already has all these plans of taking her to the beach once I'm healthy and to Disney World. I wouldn't be surprised if he comes back here with clothes and toys for her."

"He's a good man. Does he have a brother or something?"

I laughed and then I gasped in excitement. "Why didn't I think about this before?! Jordan!"

Zoe rolled her eyes. "No, no, no, you're not going to play matchmaker with me. You know I don't date white boys."

"And he happens to be into dark girls. But, I'm sure he'll make an exception," I countered.

She folded her arms over her chest. "He's funny, and I think he does something with music. He's probably trying to be a rapper." She snickered to herself. "We wouldn't have anything in common. What does he know about black culture?"

"Hmm. I'd think he'd know a lot considering that his parents are black."

"What?"

"He's adopted. But even if he was raised by white parents, it shouldn't matter."

"It matters to me."

"I'll have you know that he and Sean met in college majoring in African-American Studies. He was a double major with Music. He probably knows more about Black people than you do."

Zoe looked annoyed. "So, he's got a little thing for black people, that doesn't mean I should go out with him."

"So the only reason you don't want to go out with him is because he's white? Oh Zo, you're *such* a hypocrite."

"I'm not being a hypocrite."

"Yes, you are. I can tell what you're thinking. This guy could be the coolest guy in the world, but you don't want to date him because you're afraid to have light kids."

"My kids won't be black Anaya! They won't even *look* black. You said yourself that I could pass. Can you imagine if I had *kids* with a white guy? They'd have it even worse than I did. They'd probably pass. I couldn't handle that."

I sighed. "First of all, I need you to stop treating every man like a potential sperm donor. You should be with someone because of the way they treat you, the way they make you feel, because you love them. And with regards to kids, yeah, they'll be mixed. But, they'll still be black because *you're* black and I'm certain you'll teach them to be proud of their heritage and knowing Jordan so would he. There's nothing wrong with being biracial. It's not a curse." I shook my head. "Ironically, I'm willing to bet that Jordan would have them check Black instead of the Other box."

"So he's a white boy that wants to be black."

"No, he's a man who's racially white but was raised in a culturally African-American home. I don't think Jordan is blind. He knows he will never be classified as a black man." I sighed. "But, then again what is race? Aren't you the one who told me that race is not just simply what you look like?"

Zoe smirked at that and then looked back down. "Race is a social construct. But, it's still important. It can dictate culture. People should have a right to be culturally proud."

"They should. I am proud to be a Jamaican. But my pride, shouldn't stop me from loving an American. From embracing an American."

"So wanting to preserve my blackness shouldn't stop me from liking white people."

"Or Asians, Native Americans, Latinos-

Zoe held up her hand to stop me. "Ok, I got your point. God, I'm parroting everything my stepfather taught me."

"If I shouldn't love my kids more or less because of the color of their skin, then neither should you. And that starts with loving people regardless of their skin, their race, nationality, class- just about anything you can think of."

"I didn't realize how hard this would be."

"What?"

"Purging ourselves of these ideologies we've had." She looked out the window. "I'm sitting at this man's house with a baby in my arms and thinking he's really cute. Naya, he was even flirting with me and I was just cold... because he's white. I feel like a jerk."

"You should." I said, smiling.

"I should tell you something important."

I raised my eyebrows.

"So I have this friend who's a counselor and she hosts these youth enrichment programs all the time. She's having a self-esteem camp for young girls."

"And?"

"And I signed us up."

"What?!"

"It'll be good for us. Sean thinks it's funny, but he agrees we should do it," Zoe said.

"You got my husband in this?" I rolled my eyes

and took the brochure from her and read it. "This is a camp for teens."

"Tweens and teens."

I moved the brochure to stare at her. "Oh God, this is going to be so embarrassing."

"It will be. But, we'll be embarrassed *together*. This camp could do wonders for us. You won't know until you try."

"Where's this camp?"

"Islamorada."

"That's three hours away. I have kids Zoe."

"Kids who have a very capable father." She crossed her leg over the other. "Look, Sean already agreed to this, so I'm sure he realizes he has the kids for the week. Plus, if you don't go it'll just appear to Sean like you're not ready to work on your self-esteem and ultimately your marriage."

"Are you trying to guilt trip me?"

"Absolutely," she said, grinning mischievously.

"I can't believe this."

We sat there staring at the TV for a bit watching Candace yell at her two brothers for building a roller coaster.

"I've been thinking about maybe finding my dad," Zoe said.

She played in her curls absent-mindedly. "You know how they say that you have to deal with the root of things. Well, I'm thinking that knowing my dad might help me."

I nodded and adjusted Jeremy on my lap. "It might."

"Yeah and I talked to my stepfather and my mother on the phone last night."

My eyebrows rose. "You did? How did that go?"

Zoe rolled her eyes. "Ahhh, I don't know. But at least I got to say what I needed to say."

"And...?"

"I called and my mom picked up. She was... shocked that I had called. I mean it wasn't a holiday and, let's just say she was even more shocked that I asked for my stepfather to join in on the call."

I smiled. I can only imagine Zoe grilling her parents like witnesses on the stand. She continued,

"So I told them that I've been unhappy for majority of my life... and that it's not their fault."

"Huh?"

"I don't like playing the victim. I've been away from my parents for years and I could've made my own happiness. But I didn't. So I told them it wasn't their fault. But, I did tell them that they left me with some scars." She rested her head back against the couch and closed her eyes and for the first time, I saw tears rolling down Zoe's face. "I told my mom that I was proud of her for being a doctor, for being a professional woman. But, having a mother was more important to me than only being able to brag about her career. I was raised by babysitters. And my stepfather..."

She started to sniffle. "Well, I told him that all he preaches about is black power and that's great and all, but he treats it like it's about anger. I don't think it is."

She scratched her head. "I think it's ok to be angry about the injustices that happened before and even angry about the ones that continue to happen.

As a black woman and a lawyer, I get ticked when I hear about boys getting gunned down just because he *might* be dangerous. But, I think we've internalized that anger. Some of us walk around angry at anything and anyone. Granted, we have reasons to be, we're in a world that tells us all we're good for is singing, dancing, sports, and sex. But, I wonder how helpful all that anger is for us."

Jeremy gripped my finger. I rubbed his arm. Jeremy would grow up having to navigate himself in a world, where race still did matter, even though we'd done marches, written books, made TV specials. It mattered.

Zoe sighed. "Whether it's hatred that's been placed inside of us towards ourselves or hatred towards white people for the history of what they've done to blacks, what you and I have done to ourselves is anger bottled up inside with no outlet."

I nodded. "You're right," Jeremy began to get restless and Zoe scooped him up in her arms. "So what do we do?"

"Exactly what I told my stepfather. Let go."

"Will he let go?"

She gave Jeremy a kiss and he rested his hands filled with slob on her face. "I don't know. But, it doesn't matter anymore."

"Why not?"

"Because I'm letting go. Can't you tell by my tears Naya? I'm finally letting go."

9 HE'S GOT A NAME

"Oh na na na na na na." Jordan walked in singing the famous refrain from Beenie Man's "Romie". He always sang that to tease me. "How's my favorite yaardie?" he said, sitting on the couch. I laughed at Jordan's pathetic attempt at a Jamaican accent. Sean walked in behind him. I was in the kitchen making dinner and Sean came over and gave me a kiss.

"Ugh… get a room," Jordan said.

Sean walked up behind him and knocked him in his head. "It's my house."

"And you invited me over," Jordan said. Sean took Jeremy out of the playpen, sat down on the couch, and changed the channel. "Look at me being rude, Anaya, how have you been feeling?" He said, coming by me and giving me a hug. Every time I saw Jordan I marveled at how healthy he looked after three years of remission.

"Better."

"You look good," Jordan said. "You look happy. Sean's been looking pretty happy too," he said, winking at us.

Sean shook his head. "Watch your mouth Jordan."

"What?" he said innocently. "All I said is that ya'll look good. Like newlyweds."

I laughed.

Sean changed the topic. "Are you going to get Nadia from school soon?"

"Zoe went to pick her up so I could have some time to cook."

Jordan rolled his eyes. "Ahh, the girl who came by the crib the other day. She was not into me, Sean. I was being all friendly with this girl and she just shutdown."

"Really? Zoe seemed so funny to me when I met her," Sean said.

Ok, time for me to do damage control...and get back Zoe for this camp thing. "So, since we're talking about Zoe, Jordan I should tell you that she's single."

Jordan rolled his blue eyes again and moved back to the couch and sat down. I always thought he looked a bit like Clark Kent with a 5' o clock shadow. Those blue eyes against that dark hair. "Great, another person trying to set me up. Didn't I just tell you she seemed like she could care less about dating me?" He was wearing a plaid shirt, some jeans, boots and a tam over his head.

"Look, I could be on your case about looking like a Rastafarian lumberjack, but I'm trying to help you get with a beautiful, smart, career woman."

Sean burst out laughing and Jordan narrowed his eyes at me. "Those herbs Sean told me you take need to cure your smart mouth."

"I like her smart mouth," Sean said. Jeremy started making noises. Even Jeremy was defending me.

"So now you want to give me dating tips?"

"No, just be you. I think Zoe was just having an

off day. Approach her again."

He sighed. "She better not be crazy Naya. I think it might ruin our friendship if she is."

"She's not. She's my friend from college, she's a lawyer and really funny. Her favorite music is pretty much all from the 90's. Hip-hop. R&B."

"People always make these girls seem amazing and then I go out with them and they're crazy."

"Do you think I'd have a crazy woman living with me?"

"But, *you're* a crazy woman."

"Hey!" Sean said. "She's *my* crazy woman."

"Exactly."

I heard the door open Nadia burst into the family room and I looked from the kitchen and saw her jump on the couch next to Sean and start playing with Jeremy. Zoe appeared in the family room. She stopped short and glared at me knowingly, before smiling and greeting everyone. She made her way into the kitchen pretending to assist me in the kitchen. I smiled to myself. Zoe was nervous.

"Zoe this is Jordan. Jordan this is Zoe." I said,

while both of them gave me the eye. They turned to each other and Jordan stuck out his hand. "We've met." Jordan said, grinning at me.

Zoe shook his hand. It was firm...she was in business mode. She goes into business mode when she's nervous. *Loosen up, Zo.*

"So, Anaya tells me you're a lawyer."

"I am." Zoe was leaning forward against the counter and I moved myself behind her, out of Jordan's view and pinched her leg. "Ow!" Zoe yelled and then swatted at me. "Look, Jordan. I'm a lawyer so beating around the bush doesn't really work for me. Anaya is obviously plotting for us and will stop at nothing until she gets us alone with each other again."

I groaned and put my hand to my head. "Zoe, must you always be so blunt?"

I looked to Jordan whose eyebrows were raised in surprise and then he grinned with amusement. "I've had these two try to set me up before, but I've never had a woman *not* play along."

"I can assure you I'm not like the other women."

Sean was looking from Zoe to Jordan to me and I stayed still my eyes on Jordan to read his expression. Gosh, I probably should've told Zoe *not* to be her usual self. There was no way Jordan would go out with someone as prickly as Zoe was being. Jordan only nodded at Zoe's statement. "Can you sing?" he asked Zoe.

Her back was facing me. "Huh?" I heard her ask before she said, "I can hold a note," her voice sounding suspicious. Zoe couldn't hold a note, but Jordan would eventually figure that out.

"Do you want to go hang out in the studio?" I'm sure my face was showing the utter shock I was feeling on the inside.

"The studio?"

"Yeah, maybe record something. You can have it as a keepsake."

"So you're a rapper?" Zoe said, eyeing me.

Jordan laughed. "No, I'm a producer."

Zoe's body loosened from her tense stance before. I looked over to Sean and held a thumb up and then held up a thumb down. He looked at Zoe's face and discreetly sent me back a thumb up.

"Ok, I'll go to the studio. When?"

"We can go now or whenever you'd like."

"I'd feel bad making Anaya cook so much, only to ditch her for dinner."

"Don't feel bad," I said, loudly. I cleared my throat. "Um, I meant, it's no big deal. We'll just have leftovers. More for us."

Sean chipped in. "Yup, I can actually have some extra food to carry for my lunch."

"See, no conflict," I said to Zoe. "Make sure you record something for our retreat Zoe."

She shook her head at me and then turned back to Jordan. He shrugged and gave a boyish grin. "You said she was relentless."

"Ok," Zoe said.

Jordan gave her space to walk to the door. "After you."

Zoe walked to the door and then turned around to look at us, to which we all responded by waving at her and Sean whispered something to Nadia. Nadia replied loudly saying "Bye, Auntie Zoe have fun!"

"And be nice to Jordan!" I added.

Zoe smiled and waved back and then they were gone.

I'd put Jeremy to sleep, playing with his soft curls. I must've ran my finger softly over his face a million times. Babies are forgiving in ways adults aren't.

Nadia had also knocked out and Sean had put her in her room and then came over into Jeremy's room. "How do you think it's going?"

I sighed. "I'm praying it's going well and she isn't being her blunt self."

"Jordan can hold his own and to be honest I think he liked her bluntness."

"I sure hope so."

He came over and rubbed my arms. "Your skin feels a bit better."

"Olive Oil."

"Ahh."

We walked back over to our room.

I started to get ready for bed. "Sean can I ask

you a question?"

"Sure," he said, popping his head out the bathroom while brushing his teeth.

"You teach African- American History and I know you're... 'afrocentric'...."

He looked amused and then moved into the bathroom. I heard him spit and gargle mouthwash. He came back inside our room.

"Yeah, so I wanted to know how did you find a balance between that and not having hard feelings towards..."

"Jordan? And other white people?"

"Yeah."

He got in bed. "When I first met Jordan I was thinking what is this white boy doing in all these Black History classes? I thought maybe he felt he had something to prove. And then we got assigned to a group project together."

I sat down on the edge of the bed.

"And I got to know him and he became more than just the white boy in class. He had likes and dislikes. He had hobbies. He could sing, he could dance, he wasn't just some stereotype I had in my head. Then I went to his house for the first time and got the shock of my life when I met his parents. I mean, I definitely wasn't expecting to meet two people who looked like they belonged in *my* family."

I laughed. "I think maybe everyone has that same reaction to meeting his parents."

"I know, so then I started thinking Jordan probably has to deal with this everyday, people judging him. The same way they judge me because of my skin...and I thought, if I'm demanding respect for all the qualities I have besides my skin, my race, my ethnicity, then I have to give that same respect to Jordan, white people, Asians, Native Americans, everyone I meet."

On the days that Sean worked, 7:30 am always started my routine; I woke up, made breakfast and took Nadia to daycare. When I came back in, I put Jeremy back down for a nap and ate some breakfast and started on the laundry. The doorbell rang. Zoe was at the door. I opened up for her.

"You have a key," I said.

"I know. I left them at home." She walked inside. She was wearing the same clothes from last night.

She sat down on my sofa.

"No, you didn't Zo. Not on your first date," I said, incredulously.

She shook her head. "I didn't. We just spent hours recording and talking and laughing. I didn't even kiss him on the first date, unlike you," she teased.

I gasped and put my hand over my mouth. "So you had a good time with *the white boy*."

She smirked. "I had a great time with *Jordan*."

"Oooh and you're calling him Jordan instead of the white boy. He has a name, folks," I said, as I tickled Zoe's side and she swatted my hand away.

"You were right."

"I was what?"

"You were right."

"And did you bring up anything about kids and the future?"

"No, we just talked about our lives and I told him stuff I don't remember telling any guy before."

I raised my eyebrows. "Like what?"

"Well, he asked if I wanted to go to the beach sometime...And I said yes. But, I opened up and told him about the tanning and I thought he would run. I mean I regretted saying it as soon as it came out. But, he didn't, instead he said how about we go at sunset?"

"Ohh, Jordan's getting all romantic," I said, as I ate my French toast. "And I have no idea why I told him about the retreat."

"You did?"

"Yes, he thought it was funny that we were going to be bunking with kids and talking about our feelings, but he was supportive."

"He must really like you."

"Don't get my hopes up."

"I don't think you have reason to worry, but I won't push it full force until *after* the retreat."

"Why *after*?"

"Because by then I think we'll both be able to

look at our relationships in a healthier way. At least I hope so."

"Me too."

"So what did you record at the studio?" I asked Zoe.

She smiled. "Something educational."

"Oh God, what?"

"Lauryn Hill, Doo wop."

"That thing?"

She nodded.

I threw my head back and laughed.

10 WRITE THAT DOWN

As the bus rolled down US1 towards Islamorada, I realized I'd made a mistake agreeing to this camp while my body was still recouping. I felt stiff. I kept shifting myself to stretch.

"You ok?" Zoe asked.

"I'm fine, just a bit stiff," I said over the chitter chatter of all the girls in the bus. They ranged from middle school to high school girls. Some were blond, some had thick curly hair, some had their kinky hair sprouting into the air, braids and relaxed hair falling onto their shoulders. Some had faint scarring on the insides of their wrists, on their thighs, others had the shortest and tightest clothes possible.

Personalities seemed easy to read on a bus full of girls. There were those who turned to each other, talking loudly, popping their gum. Others opted for headphones, texted, zoned out and slept. Then there were the few who scattered among the riders who were hunched over a book. I smiled inwardly. Rachel Ulysses, was the director of the program and a friend of Zoe's. She was going around the bus and giving out room assignments, now that we were about 30 minutes away from our destination. She came by and greeted us. She placed her hand on our seats and the row ahead of ours.

"Young ladies," she said to the row ahead of us. "These are your roommates, get to know them," she said walking off.

"Hey are you gonna be our teachers?"

Both Zoe and I looked up to see two chubby cheeked girls staring down at us. They had turned in their seats, breaking the rules to stay buckled up. They rested their arms against the top of their seats. One was Hispanic, wearing a bracelet with the Cuban flag proudly displayed on it. Her curly hair was pulled back away from her face that looked a bit like those baby angels you see in paintings. The next one was a black girl wearing glasses, her hair in a large afro.

"No, sweetie, we're going to do the camp with you guys."

Both made a face. "You're too old to do the camp," the Hispanic girl said.

"How old do you think I am?"

"I don't know," the Hispanic one said.

"Maybe forty," the black one said.

"Forty!" Zoe said, and my jaw dropped.

Zoe leaned back against her seat. "What's your names?" she asked both girls.

"My name's Mia and she's Savannah," the Hispanic one answered.

"Those are pretty names. Mia and Savannah. My name is Zoe and this is my friend Anaya." Zoe unbuckled her seatbelt. "Let's get one thing straight. I'm only thirty two."

"Well, you're technically almost thirty three," I whispered.

Zoe scowled at me.

"What? It's true." I said, innocently.

Zoe turned back to the girls. "Yes, we're a little too old to be on this trip, but we need to work on some stuff just as much as you do. So make sure you tell all your little friends to get as much as they can from this retreat pumpkin, or else you'll end up like us. Thirty two and on a trip with 12 year olds."

Both girls stared at us before turning away and sitting down in their seats.

I leaned sideways, close to Zoe. "I don't think I feel better about this situation after that little speech."

"Neither do I, but I think we stuck up for ourselves, don't you?"

I shook my head in disbelief. "You're worried about being bullied by some kids?" I whispered fast.

"Yes, aren't you?" she whispered back.

"It hadn't crossed my mind Zo, especially since I'm a grown woman."

"Well, you better start thinking about it considering there are over fifty of them and two of us."

"You cannot be serious," I said, laughing.

"Kids are ruthless nowadays Naya. Think about it, girls who have self-esteem problems often prey on the insecurities of others." She took a peek through the slit in between the seats at Mia and Savannah. "Those two are going to try to have a field day with us."

"That's it. You're officially crazy." I said, turning my eyes to the window to look at the blue of the Atlantic zipping by.

"Mark my words, Naya. Watch your back. These two are not to be trifled with."

Thirty minutes later we got to our destination, the wooden beach houses painted in yellows, oranges and blues. Each house was given a housemother who was actually probably younger than Zoe and I. We were assigned to beach house #1, the blue one., room 4. We were only allowed to give one call back home to let them know we'd reached safely. Then all cellphones had to be turned in. Our families had the number to call our housemother in case of an emergency. I huffed at Zoe about that. I wanted to check in on Sean and the kids daily. I was just getting my time back with Jeremy and watching him and Nadia interact with each other.

"Hey girls, it's three pm right now. We have a group session at seven tonight. So catch a nap and be ready on time," Alex, our house mother said to us. She was a petite redhead, although I'm unsure if it was dye or her natural color.

Zoe rolled my suitcase for me while I held onto the banister carefully climbing the stairs.

"What's wrong old lady?"

I turned around to see Savannah and Mia standing behind me, their duffel bags in hand. They both smiled and then pushed ahead of us into our room. I turned to Zoe, my face straight.

"Mi nuh believe dis," I said slightly out of breath.

"Believe it," Zoe said.

"Dem nuh know seh mi spank pickney?"

"Ok, you lost me. Translation?" Zoe asked.

"I will spank them kids."

Zoe smiled. "Well, we can't spank, but we can still teach them how to mind their elders."

"Agreed."

We finished walking up the stairs. It took me longer than Zoe because I was careful to stretch too much or move too fast. The room had a bunk bed and two double beds inside. Mia and Savannah had already secured the bunk beds. Good, I didn't want that anyway. I grabbed the bed closest to the bathroom.

Both Mia and Savannah sat there staring down at us. "Are you guys going to nap?" Savannah asked.

"Yeah, you know how older people need to nap," Mia chirped.

"As a matter of fact, I am."

"Whoa," Savannah said. "You're from Jamaica?"

I realized Zoe had done most of the talking and they hadn't heard me. "Yes."

"How come you don't have dreads?"

"Do you two always ask rude questions?" Zoe snapped.

"Zoe, it's straight." I turned to the girls. "Not

every Jamaican has dreads and I move slowly because I have a skin condition right now. My skin is super sensitive, it can tear or bruise pretty easily."

Their faces registered surprise. "You're lying," Mia said. "You're just trying to make us feel bad."

"Nope," I said, showing them the insides of my arms to show them the scar from the stitches. "So I actually need some rest, because for a few weeks I've been having to take care of both my kids with all these problems."

Their little faces looked actually stricken. "We're sorry. I mean we didn't-"

I held up a hand. "It's ok. Zoe and I are cool, I promise, we're going to have lots of fun if we can get along." They looked at Zoe, who was still looking a bit angry, leaned back against the bed rest, her arms folded across her chest. "So can we call a truce?" I asked them.

They turned away from us and whispered among themselves. After a couple seconds they turned back to us. "Ok, truce."

I looked at Zoe. "Zoe, do you agree to the truce?"

Zoe eyed me. "Ok," she said grudgingly.

I got up to walk towards the bathroom.

"Wait!" Mia and Savannah yelled.

I froze.

"I think we should wipe up the floors first," Mia said, getting down off of the top bunk.

"What did you guys do to it?" I asked.

"We kinda rubbed baby oil on it," Savannah said.

My mouth was wide open when I turned around to Zoe who just shook her head and plopped down on the bed, curly hair flying upward.

The girls let Zoe and I rest peacefully and when I woke up at 6:15, I saw that they had actually fallen asleep as well. I freshened up and got dressed. Rousing the girls and Zoe awake, I told them to get dressed so we could eat before the next session.

Watching them rub their eyes reminded me how young they actually were even though they thought they were 12 going on 21. I reminded them to brush their teeth and wash their faces before coming downstairs.

"I'm going to get us some food," I said. "Hurry. It's already 6:30."

Zoe smiled. "You're in your element."

"What do you mean?"

"You're being a mother."

The session later was outside on the beach, the sun lazy and low in the sky. It created a red glow across the horizon that sent pink and purple clouds across the sky. The waves were strong and despite Rachel's teaching I sat there thinking, there has to be a God.

"We're going to do something a bit different than usual. I'm going to hand out a journal to each of you and I want you to write down every negative thing you believe about yourself that comes to your mind. Right now, we're going to write down every negative thing," Rachel said.

Zoe leaned close and whispered. "Isn't that a bit counterproductive? Shouldn't we find the positive first?"

"It might be harder for these girls as well as for

us to think of twenty good things. But, it's much easier to find twenty bad things...I don't know Zo, just do it."

We both started writing in our notebooks. I scribbled in my notebook:

1. *I have stretch marks all over and fragile skin*
2. *My skin is as dark as night*

I thought of writing that I wished I had different color eyes, but then I thought of what Sean had said about them looking like coffee.

3. *My thighs rub.*
4. *I hate how my underarms are permanently tinted.*
5. *I'm impatient*
6. *I'm a bad mother*
7. *I wish I wasn't so insecure. I wish didn't compare myself to others.*

I had finished writing and looked up. The lists on others notebooks, looked far longer than mine. I mean I had thought I'd end up writing more, but the weight of what I'd written had been sufficient.

"Two more minutes," Rachel called out.

I secretly wanted to peek at what Zoe had written, but that would be invasive. I tapped my thumb.

"Ok, finish up girls," Rachel said, and the pens started to slow down until they eventually stopped.

"Ok, so throughout this week I want you to work towards replacing those negative things you wrote about yourself with positives that cancels out those negative feelings. Also, every time you say something negative about yourself, I want you to write it down. I want you to realize how many times a day you speak something negative over yourself."

I looked around at the group of young girls, their faces all uniquely captivating. Whether it was the flecks of color in their eyes, the shade of their skin, the cute mole near their mouth, all of them looked different and somehow...perfect. Some were probably writing that they were too fat, too skinny, too flat-chested, too busty, hippy, hipless, all sorts of nonsense. I thought about what Zoe said to Mia and Savannah in the bus. It was true. This retreat could help them not to be 32 year olds sitting in the sand wondering which was the true cancer, melanoma or self-hatred.

We all had a bonfire on the beach, making smores, which was new for me. I'd never made smores before. But, I'd rather had come back to my room smelling like smoke because I'd roasted some fish. Zoe told me my Jamaican side was showing.

"What other side am I supposed to show?" I joked.

We all went back to the room and washed again, trying to get the smoky smell off our bodies and out our hair.

I went in first, then Zoe, Mia, and Savannah. "I don't know how to comb through this thing," Savannah said. "My hair sucks. It'd be better if it was like Mia's."

"No, my hair's horrible, it'd be better if it was

straight, then I wouldn't have to-"

"Whoa," Zoe said. "Both of you have great hair. And both of you should write down what you said in your journals.

Mia and Savannah moped over to their beds and grabbed their journals.

"We can help you, you know," I said. "With your hair."

"Can you?"

"Yeah."

"Bring that comb over here, Savannah," Zoe said. "Do you have any more of that coconut oil Naya?"

"Yeah," I said, grabbing some out of my suitcase. "Do you have any of that leave in conditioner and that gel thing you use in your hair for definition?"

Zoe grabbed the two bottles out of her bag and threw them in my direction. "Mia, dampen your hair again and come, I'll help you out."

Mia wet her hair, came over, and sat on my bed, her back to me and her legs crisscrossed in front of her. I took another comb and began to comb gently through the curls.

"My mom always complains about doing my hair. She just sends me to the hairdresser and makes them straighten it whenever she gets fed up."

"Your mom should recognize that you've got a treasure with all these thick curls."

She snorted, as if to refute what I was saying, but then kept quiet.

"I'm serious. You can do anything with this hair. Have it curly, have it straight. It doesn't matter whether you choose to wear it straight or curly. But I don't want you to hate your hair. It's beautiful."

I looked over to see Zoe starting to give Savannah twists similar to what she had given Nadia. I missed Nadia.

"What's something you put on your list Ms. Anaya?" Mia asked me.

"I'll spill if you spill."

"Ok, I put that I think I'm fat. My mom and Abuela are always telling me I need to stop eating so much."

God, I felt bad for this girl. Being actually surrounded by negativity. I mean the negative thoughts I had about myself, I'd mostly done those to myself through comparing myself to everyone, including movie stars. I hadn't really had any family outright tell me there was something wrong with me.

"You look beautiful, Mia," and I meant that. Mia was 12 and still had chubby cheeks, but that was it. I thought they made her look angelic, not fat. "Eat whatever you want. Actually, no I shouldn't tell you that as a doctor," I said laughing. "It's important to eat healthy. But, it's not healthy to obsess over weight."

Mia nodded. "So, what did you put in yours?"

I saw Zoe look over at me. I sighed. "I put that I didn't like my skin."

"What about it?"

"I think it's too dark."

Savannah eyes locked onto mine, even though she was supposed to be holding her head still for Zoe to work. "No, Ms. Anaya, it's perfect."

"Yeah, Ms. Anaya. You remind me of that new actress that just won the Oscar."

"Lupita?" Zoe asked.

"Yeah," Savannah gushed. "She does."

"And you know she just won Most Beautiful in this magazine. So you're in good company," Mia said.

I smiled in spite of myself. "You really think so?"

"Yeah, my mom is from Tanzania and she used to tell me these bedtime stories about princesses from her country. I bet one of them looked like you."

"Thank you," I said, feeling a weight lift off of me. I should write this new positive in my notebook. "I should probably get your mother to send me that story, so I can tell it to my daughter."

Savannah's face read sadness. "She's dead. She died two years ago. That's why I have no one to help me with my hair."

"Oh, I'm sorry sweetie," I said, finishing off a long braid down Mia's back.

Zoe hugged Savannah. "Well, we're here to do it now, and you're going to look so fly. And I'm going to teach you how to do some stuff to it, so that when you go home, it won't be so hard anymore, ok?"

Savannah nodded. "I wrote about my hair in my

journal. It was the thing I disliked, but my dad won't let me get a perm yet."

"You won't need one when I'm done teaching you this week," Zoe said.

Mia hugged a pillow to her chest. "Ok, Ms. Zoe, your turn."

Zoe pointed at herself. "Me?"

"Yeah, you," Savannah giggled, still leaning over, letting Zoe twist her hair.

"Uhh... well, what do you guys think I am? Black, white, or Hispanic?"

"Uhh, I dunno Savannah said, "I think you're mixed."

"Yeah, like my cousin Kelly," Mia said.

"Well, I'm not, both of my parents are black. But no one ever thinks I am. So, sometimes I get upset about that."

"Oh..." Savannah said, "Well, what does it matter? You're black regardless."

"Exactly," Mia said. "Some people got real mad, when my aunt Maite married this black guy. But he's the best. They thought her kids wouldn't be Cuban anymore. But, my cousin *is* Cuban *and* she's black."

"Do you think it makes people in your family or at school treat her differently?" Zoe asked Mia.

"Yeah, some people in the family complain about her curly hair, like they complain about mine, or that her skin is brown. Sometimes people at school will tease her too. But, I've fought a kid for her, I don't care that she's both Cuban and Black and neither does she."

"Why not?

Mia struggled for words and then just shrugged. "I dunno, she knows she's fly."

Zoe's eyes widened and then she laughed. "She knows she's fly. I like that."

Savannah chimed in. "Yeah, once my dad was trying to explain that stuff to me. He got a big bottle of chocolate syrup and a glass of milk. He was like, 'Vanna chocolate syrup tastes good on its own and so does milk, but there ain't nothing wrong with sometimes mixing them together. It can taste just as good.'"

I looked over at Zoe, I think the kids said it all

tonight. I had better write this down.

The next few days were a whirlwind of sisterhood exercises, sex education for the girls, and several forced awkward moments looking in the mirror and giving ourselves self-affirming words. Zoe and I made sure we had our own sessions with Mia and Savannah, which Zoe made sure included listening to No Scrubs, That Thing, and India Aire. We taught them how to do the Kid 'n Play, Bogle, Tootsie Roll and they taught us how to dougie and nae nae. They begged me to teach them how to do Jamaican dancehall moves, but even I knew that would be a bad idea for two twelve year olds. We'd had fun and despite our ages and different families, we felt like sisters.

"What do you want to be when you grow up girls?" Zoe asked three days later as we all walked on the beach at sunset, all sucking on different popsicles, they'd given out earlier. Even though it was sunset, I wore sunscreen and a long sleeved shirt and pants. I couldn't risk any more melanomas. Those stitches had hurt.

"I used to want to be a model, mostly because I wanted to be skinny," Mia said. "But, I think I want to be a scientist or something. I mean I'm smart. I just didn't try too hard in school."

"Ok, scientist by day, Selena Gomez look-a-like by night," I said. Mia gushed at that.

"How about you Savannah?" I asked.

"I want to be a teacher, like my mom was."

"Yes!" Zoe said, giving her a high five.

I realized that all of us had to write down that we'd said something negative, less and less.

"I don't want this week to end," Savannah said.

Neither do I., well; except I wanted to go home to my family, but if my family could've been here with me, I would never leave. But, even I know that no one can live on the mountaintop forever. I had to return to my life and deal with the challenges.

"Me neither. But, I think the only way we'll know if this retreat was any good is when we go back.

Because then we'll face all the things that used to bring us down and we'll have to choose how we'll handle it," Zoe said.

Both Mia and Savannah nodded and kept walking, the wind blowing their hair and clothes.

"When I get home I'm going to show my dad all the new stuff you and Anaya taught me to do with my hair. And that boy that called me ugly at school, me and Mia are gonna jump him."

"Savannah," I said.

"I'm just kidding," she said. "You're so easy to get. I'm just gonna give him a piece of my mind."

"Intelligently and respectfully," Zoe said.

"Yeah, we won't curse or nothing," Mia said.

"Good," Zoe said. "You can express yourselves without it."

"I'm going to tell my mom to buy me those hair products. They've made my hair so much better. And I'm going to eat ice cream in front of my mom too."

"Don't be rude to your mom," I said, amused.

"I won't be. But, I just want her to know that I'm not fat."

"Remember that it matters more what you think of yourself than what she thinks of you."

"Right," She said, her lips red, from her cherry flavored treat.

"Zo, what are you going to do when you get home? It better involve a certain music producer."

Zoe stuck out a purple tongue at me. "It might. But, more importantly it involves me not being angry anymore. I'm going to try to find my father. Maybe have some sort of closure in that area. Thank you Mia and Savannah for those stories you told me the first night. They gave me a lot to think about."

"Just remember that you're fly, Ms. Zoe," Mia said.

Zoe cradled Mia's face in her hands, squeezing her cheeks. "I will *always* remember that."

I smiled. Savannah bit a piece of her blue popsicle. "What are you going to do Ms. Naya?"

"I'm going home to my children and my husband. And I'm going to say sorry to my husband for being horrible for so long. I'm going to kiss my son. I'm going to tell my daughter she's the prettiest girl in the world…. for once I'm actually going to be happy."

All three of them looked at me, smiled and then engulfed me in a hug. I mouthed to Zoe, "Thank you."

11 IT STILL EXISTS

Time was moving along for us. Being home felt amazing in ways that were hard to express. I could stretch now and my skin looked much better. It had a certain glow to it. The scars from all the tears and melanomas still remained, but I'd dodged a bullet. There was still no sign of cancer in my body.

Leaving behind the beach house, Mia, and Savannah, six months ago, had been hard. I don't remember feeling such sadness at leaving a place, since I left Jamaica. Zoe and I called both of them regularly and invited them out or over the house to play with my kids. Nadia loved them and both Mia and Savannah were just in love with Jeremy, who was becoming a handful now that he could walk.

Nadia's fourth birthday was approaching and we began to plan a trip to Jamaica to visit my family. Sean had only been there once, Julie's funeral, and phone calls to my parents weren't cutting it anymore. I wanted to go back to my homeland.

Sean and I were adjusting back to life with each other. I smiled more. We smiled more. And I was thinking that maybe I needed to pay a visit to the OB/GYN to check if I was expecting again. I was nervous to put my skin through all of the rigors of pregnancy again, but I believed that if that test came back positive then God would give me the strength to make it through another pregnancy...and some herbs, teas, and cocoa butter.

I'd started going back to work slowly, but then decided to still take another year off to rest and take care of my kids. Zoe and I did our daily affirmations. Some were scriptures or quotes. Some days we just prayed for one another and other days we did self-reflections, and wrote letters to ourselves or to God. I never noticed how much lies I believed until I wrote them down and read them aloud. More and more Zoe and I were realizing that the beauty that counted was the one we are often blind to.

Each time I hear Jeremy coo, or Nadia runs to me, a smile on her face, I say thanks that my silent request to God for these perfect light children had been given a resounding no. My kids were still perfect with their chocolate colored skin. If my kids still lived in a world that would not value them for the "content of their character", the world would suffer a great loss. But, my kids would not live in despair because of it. Every day I had to affirm them, because the world might not. I'd have to remind my son that he could be anything he wanted to be. That he would be a great father, a great leader. I'd have to tell Nadia that she was beautiful, even if she was underrepresented in the media, or a rapper told her she'd be better if she were "red". And I'd have to tell myself that I am so much more than this shell of skin. I am a heart, a mind, a spirit and a soul.

Zoe had connected with her father in Chicago. He was shocked to find out she even existed, and Zoe was happy to find out she had a brother and a sister. She'd met them and they were going to come down here for Thanksgiving. She and Jordan actually started seeing each other, and just like I predicted, they hit it off. Sean and I are guessing he'll propose this winter. Zoe even gave me a thank you card for setting them up, which I had framed and put in my office so that both of us would never forget.

We were in the car on our way to the beach with Zoe and Jordan. Sean and I were in the car talking about the flight arrangements for going to Jamaica in December when we heard Nadia in the back singing.

"Sing it loud, I'm black and I'm proud!"

"Where did you learn that?" Sean said, amused.

"Auntie Zoe and Uncle Jordan."

I laughed and Sean found the song on his IPod, playing it in the car for the remaining drive to Key Biscayne.

Both Zoe and I lathered ourselves in sunscreen. She'd escaped a cancer diagnosis, but we both wanted it to stay that way. Even Sean and Jordan covered themselves in it too even though it was close to sunset. I'm not sure if they did it as an act of solidarity or if our health circumstances had driven fear into them.

Nadia was just too happy to wear her new swimsuit that Zoe got for her. It was bright yellow and stylishly designed like something from the 50's, and made her skin glow. And everything was "Daddy this" and "Daddy that". I think she likes saying it so much because she's never gotten to say it before. Not to mention that Sean dotes on her. They watch movies, he reads to her and he's her favorite when it comes to playing. I'm the disciplinarian.

I'm not sure if I've ever seen Sean this happy. I mean, we've both had to adjust back to life with each other and life with two children. We have to wake up earlier, our bubble baths and late night talks get interrupted by a three year old, and then there are the new foods and clothes we have to buy for Nadia. I sat under the beach umbrella with my wide straw hat, looking like a tourist. I couldn't help but smile at Sean carrying Nadia on his shoulders into the water. Zoe and Jordan were playing with Jeremy. Jeremy giggled as Zoe dunked his chubby legs in the water.

Sean turned around and look at me, and Nadia atop his shoulders waved at me screaming, "Mommy, look!"

I waved back and thought of Julie. We'd started going through with the adoption, and I was reminded again that Nadia had been in foster care for two years before I was contacted to come and take care of her. I realized that each day, that the memory of Julie would become more faint in Nadia's mind. As much as I loved hearing her call me Mommy, I wasn't her biological mother. Julie was. And I'd promised to not let Nadia forget about her.

But she would never remember her mother. Julie had died when she was only one. I didn't even have any recent pictures to show her. I only had one picture and that was an old picture of Julie when she was 14, one month before she left. So, I'd resorted to telling her stories about Julie, singing her favorite songs, and true to the spirit of her mother, her favorite Jamaican song was Mango Time. She loved it so much that she begged us to buy her mangoes and then became fixated on them. Each day I'd cut it up and put it in her lunch pail, and remind the teachers to refrigerate it before it stunk up the whole place. Eventually, Sean had sought out a tree to plant in the backyard. But he's a city boy, so he knew nothing about planting a tree and we'd done it together. I hoped the tree would grow with her and that every mango season; she'd have a reminder of her mother.

Jordan came over and sat next to me under the umbrella. We sat there both watching Zoe.

"She looks beautiful," I said.

He nodded, still not taking his eyes off of her. The scar underneath his collarbone was still there from where his port used to be during his chemotherapy.

"Proposing soon?" I asked.

He rolled his eyes. "Sean and now you. You two are a match made in heaven."

"I know, he's the saltfish in my ackee," I said.

"You're a mess." Jordan laughed. "Actually, I have something I want to talk to you about," he said, finally looking at me.

"Ok, what's going on?"

"I was in the studio with Zoe and one of my artists walks in and Zoe leaves to go to work. So my partner starts asking if that's my girl. 'I told him yeah.'"

"I'm not understanding..." I said.

"Then he says to me, you really shouldn't mess around with them lightskins. They're too *demanding*. Get with a darkskin who doesn't have much self-esteem. She'll let you do whatever. You can cheat on her and she'll stay."

I shook my head and reached into the cooler and passed him a bottle of water and got one for myself.

"Naya. This still exists," he said, as I handed him the bottle.

"Yes, Jordan, it does."

He cracked his knuckles. "I sent him out of the studio."

"You lost business."

"I don't care. If more people started standing up for things like that, maybe people would change their-"

"Change what they say, or change their mind?"

Jordan leaned back and rested on his elbows.

"People's hearts need to be changed Jordan and that's no easy task. I'm positive Sean told you a few things about me. I was just as foolish as that guy. Knowledge is power. Awareness can mean everything."

"I learned this in school with Sean. I saw this with people's reactions to my parents."

He gulped down some of the water and watched the waves for a little while. "You know what's interesting? People get upset when you talk about white privilege, but it's real. I can avoid a lot of problems that my parents, you, Sean, and Zoe have to deal with. But people, don't know that the most important people in my life *are* black. So, I've always felt like I'm some kind of spy. I hear all the things people say when black people aren't around."

"Hmm...I think we all can be spies. I mean I hear the things people say when white people aren't around."

Jordan gave out a dry laugh. "You think I should write an expose?"

"I don't think it'd be news to most people."

"If people started talking about this in music, it would spread."

"It would. But would it spread as much as the music about thug life and sex?"

"Wouldn't know until we tried."

I held my hat against the wind. "Well then, do it. Convince some artists to work on it with you."

"I will." He started brushing at the sand on him. "I think Zoe might like helping me with it too."

"Not the singing part, right?"

"What's wrong with her voice?"

"I guess love is blind and deaf."

He laughed. "Stop hatin."

"Zoe and I are just learning to love ourselves and as time goes by it becomes easier. But, you wanna know something Jordan? I think... I think this color thing is so...futile." I drank from my bottle again. "I mean, we spend so much time claiming shades. Light skin, dark skin, brown skin, white, and at the end of it, what does it profit?"

"So should differences not matter? Do you think

we should have a 'color-blind' or a raceless society Naya?"

"When Zoe and I went to the Keys, I remember looking at all those girls and thinking that all of us looked different. Differences do matter, and as long as they matter, race and color will always matter. But, they should be appreciated, they should be celebrated. Using those differences to divide and destroy one another, is a slap in the face of the one who created all those differences to begin with."

We both looked out at Sean and Nadia now seated in the sand, Nadia scooping sand into a bucket to make a sandcastle. Zoe sat next to them, Jeremy in her lap, Jeremy clapping happily.

"And when God saw everything he made, and behold, it was very good," Jordan said.

So Jordan does pay attention in church. I looked up at the expanse of the sky. At Sean, Nadia, Jeremy, Zoe, and back at Jordan. My eyes caught my reflection in his sunglasses and I smiled.

"Exactly."

ABOUT THE AUTHOR

Shaida Escoffery- Born in Brooklyn, NY, to Jamaican parents and raised in Miami, FL was the recipient of the 2013 Atlantic Coast Conference Innovation and Creativity Fellowship for her writing at the University of Miami. This allowed her to publish her first novel *Idle, Wild, Love.* She is an alumna of the University of Miami. *Light Brights and Darkies* is her second publication.